Welcome to Sparkwood ...

where the drinks are cold, the eye candy hot, and the gossip is truly noteworthy.

Asher Hammond

I have a very big problem … in the form of one very petite woman.

Don't get me wrong. I adore women, and if you ask any female in Sparkwood, you'll learn the feeling is mutual.

With one tiny exception.

Oriana Thorne is a literal thorn in my side—a plucky, infuriatingly gorgeous, pain in the rear who rents the store next to mine.

We've disliked each other from the beginning, or at least since she marched into my shop and started issuing demands. Needless to say, I didn't roll out the welcome mat after that meet-hate.

I'd love to avoid the woman until the end of my days, but as fate would have it, I need her help.

Without her approval, my plan to open a speakeasy beneath our shops is dead in the water.

Considering Oriana is as fond of me as I am of her, winning her assistance will be no easy feat.

So, when a faulty lock forces the two of us to spend the

night together, it's anyone's guess if we'll survive until morning.

But that's a chance I'm willing to take. What's the worst that can happen?

It's not like I'm going to fall in love with the woman …

The First Spark

Sparkwood: Scenes From A Small Town
Book 1

M.L. Broome

Copyright

The First Spark

Sparkwood: Scenes From A Small Town

Copyright © 2024 by Julie E. Soper.

Cover design by Shower of Schmidt Designs

Formatting by TerraCotta Dragon Arts

To the tattooed heartbreakers who think they run the show—and the fierce, bookish women who bring them to their knees, one page at a time.

Chapter 1

The Thorn in My Side

Ash

"Ash, you *know* the rules. You need the approval of the other tenant. According to the lease, it's a shared space."

I scrub my face with my hands, releasing a sound somewhere between a groan and a growl, primarily because that is *not* the answer I want to hear. "Give me anything else—a hike through the Mojave at high noon, a quick swim in a vat of sea snakes, Russian roulette with bullets in every chamber—just don't tell me I have to work a deal with *her.*"

"Contrary to what you think, Oriana is a lovely woman."

Glancing up, I catch Kiki's smirk. Glad she's enjoying my predicament.

"Like hell she is. She's a snob who thinks she's better than us inked hoodlums."

I'm not kidding. For the past six months, Oriana Thorne has been a literal thorn in my side, ever since the day she moved next door to my tattoo parlor, Black Lotus.

At first, the woman intrigued me. After renting the

rundown space beside me, a renovation crew gutted the entire thing, turning the dank hovel into a bookstore, complete with a gourmet coffee bar and a stage for open-mic nights.

It was a night and day difference.

Anyone who owns a small business knows that vacant shops adjacent to yours are *not* a good calling card. No matter how successful *your* business may be, a half-empty strip mall screams of unstable financial futures. So, it thrilled me to have a new neighbor.

Plus, it didn't hurt that Oriana was damn easy on the eyes. She was adorable—a tiny wisp of a woman with long dark hair and enormous eyes hidden behind glasses. She was an offbeat mix of rockabilly and geeky chic, with a killer body to boot.

Things were looking up.

Until they weren't.

I planned to stroll into her store and welcome her to the neighborhood. Maybe even offer to buy her a drink at the local watering hole.

That's how it is in small towns, and I'm a lifer here in Sparkwood. I know every inch of this sleepy mountain hamlet, so named because it has views which would make Ansel Adams weep.

The beauty of the area comes with a high sticker price, so locals hang on to their property with every ounce of strength they possess. They're also wary of newcomers, but that comes with the territory.

My brother Braden and I took over our parents' micro farm when they tired of New York winters and headed for the sunny shores of Florida.

Since we had no desire to deal with humidity or alligators, we stayed put and kept the farm open and running.

But farming, despite being my birthright, wasn't my passion. Ever since I was a kid, I had been obsessed with the art of tattooing and spent years honing my skills. My parents shook their head at my career choice, but they never stopped me from pursuing my dream.

They're awesome like that. Hell, they even footed the bill for me to attend college in Manhattan and obtain a fine arts degree. I dedicated the days to the masters, but at night, I studied a different type of artistic genius—apprenticing at some of the hottest tattoo parlors in the city.

After four years, I was ready to return to Sparkwood. It just so happened that's when my folks decided to move, so I set up camp at the family homestead and opened Black Lotus.

Some artists I knew from my Manhattan days flocked to the parlor, eager for an opportunity to work as visiting artists. After six months, two of them stayed on permanently.

It didn't take long for the word to get out that there was a new name in tattooing—mine. I insisted upon the utmost in quality and professionalism from the artists in my employ, and my strict standards paid off.

Black Lotus has an impeccable reputation. My parlor isn't some backdoor chop shop. It's art on skin.

It's been a mainstay in Sparkwood for over a decade now, drawing tattoo aficionados from across the globe, all clamoring for ink.

But that's not the crux of the matter.

I'm not only a successful business owner, but I'm also a

likable guy—the type who helps ladies with their groceries or plays ball with the neighborhood kids.

In *all* my years here, I've never heard a negative word spoken against me, my artists, or my tattoo parlor—until Oriana arrived. Apparently, all she saw was a bunch of burly men covered in ink and piercings, and *that* was enough to sway her opinion.

Our introduction was the antithesis of a meet cute. It was a meet-hate instigated by Ms. Tight Ass herself when she marched into my shop, complaining about the noise.

I hadn't even had a chance to say hello, but that didn't stop Oriana from reading me the riot act. All I could do was stare at this tiny woman, her hands waving wildly, as she insinuated we were showing her patrons a total lack of respect by playing our music at an undesirable level.

Look, I admit that before she moved in, we blasted the radio after hours. Our clients didn't mind and there were no neighbors to complain.

But the day Oriana's store opened, I informed my employees to cut the volume to a respectable level.

See? I'm a nice guy. I strive for everyone to work together.

Seems that wasn't enough for our new resident pain in the ass.

Not by a long shot.

Oriana wouldn't let me get a word in edgewise during her onslaught, but when she threatened me with the town's noise ordinance, I had to laugh.

The chief of police is not only one of my best clients, but he's also a lifelong friend. When I *gently* mentioned this fact, Oriana's eyes widened, but she refused to back down an inch.

Turns out, she didn't care if my lifelong buddy was the King of England.

Instead, she segued to her next complaint, and *this* one garnered my full attention.

She wagged her finger under my nose—quite a feat, considering the height difference—and spat out that despite my reputation for being a nice person in Sparkwood, it was all bullshit. She knew what I'd said about her. It wasn't appreciated, and it would most definitely be remembered. If I wanted to play hardball, she was ready.

Then she turned and left the parlor, her petulant pout intact.

That was my introduction to Oriana Thorne. Let me tell you, after that, she was my new nemesis.

I don't take kindly to threats or insinuations that me and my guys are delinquents. She didn't say it was because our skin was inked and pierced, but come on, it's not an enormous leap.

There will always be people who judge you based on their misconceptions. I just never thought it would be my new work neighbor. Hell, she knew what type of establishment Black Lotus was when she rented the adjacent shop. Did she think we sat around sipping tea and eating crumpets?

Normally, I keep my temper shelved. At well over six feet, I'm a big guy. I'm intimidating without ever opening my mouth. But Oriana started this war, and I was damn certain to finish it.

She expected a menace to society. I'd show her one.

Five minutes later, I stormed into her bookstore, my black boots echoing on the wood floor, my hands clenched into fists.

No, I wasn't going to hit her. I'm not *that* kind of guy, and any man who is needs to be shot. But she had riled my temper, and I was determined to return the favor.

And I did, right in front of several of her patrons.

Did I feel vindicated berating a tiny woman who's half my size?

Damn right I did. She started it with her baseless accusations about me and my staff.

Fine, I also felt terrible, because, despite Oriana's belief otherwise, I care what people think of me. I've never experienced such a level of loathing from a total stranger.

Not once in all of my thirty-eight years.

Safe to say, after our blowout, there was no chance we'd be going for a welcome to the neighborhood cocktail.

In fact, I haven't heard a peep from 'Little Miss Stick Up Her Ass' in six months.

Not one word since that day.

We practice avoidance, and after all this time, we're damn good at it, too. On the off chance we're ever in the same space, there is no cordial nod or wave hello.

I toss a glare in her direction, and she returns my greeting with one of her own. That's the extent of our relationship, and even those moments are few and far between.

Trust me, I do my damnedest to ensure I'm never in the same space with Oriana, but now, our *shared* real estate space is my biggest headache.

My plan, long before Oriana arrived in Sparkwood, was to open a speakeasy establishment beneath the tattoo parlor. It was perfect, considering it *was* a speakeasy during Prohibition. Hell, the original oak bar still stands along one wall, and there are piles of memorabilia from back in the day sitting in boxes on dust-laden shelves.

I want to recapture the glitz of the Roaring '20s, complete with a historically accurate food and drink menu. There will be music, dancing, the works. Although I may not look it, I'm a huge fan of the Gatsby era.

Bonus: it's prime real estate, right on Main Street. That alone carries clout for any new venture, and I have the funds at the ready for the renovations. Top of the line everything.

Do it right or don't do it at all.

My *only* issue?

The pint-sized priss standing between me and my dream. You see, the space that both her bookstore, One More Page, and my tattoo parlor occupy used to be one unit. The owners divided the space decades ago, but only on the street-level. The basement area was to remain a shared space between the tenants.

Until now, it's never been an issue. Black Lotus stores extra supplies and equipment down there, and from what I can tell, so does Oriana.

But I need her consent before I can commence with the renovation of the space. Without her signature, I'm going nowhere fast.

Now you see why I'd rather hike the Mojave at high noon.

I huff out another groan as I crack my knuckles in frustration, my booted feet drumming against the floor. "Fuck my life. Come on, Kiki—there must be a way around this."

As owner of the strip mall, Kiki also owns the power to change the rules. Hell, just *bend* them a bit—in my favor, of course.

Kiki shakes her head as she closes her briefcase. "Ash, you knew the stipulation when you signed the lease. I even asked if you thought it would be an issue, and if you recall, you said it would *not* be a problem."

"That was when the space next door was empty."

Kiki fixes her dark gray gaze on me. "You're going to have to do better than that lame excuse."

"Can't you make an exception for me?" I shoot her my most charming smile, the one which makes the women of Sparkwood melt.

Hey, when you've got it, flaunt it, right?

I've lost count of how many women fuss over my looks. According to them, I'm the perfect combination—a muscled bad boy with the face of an angel. Throw in a plethora of ink, a neatly trimmed beard, and my Harley Road King, and you've got the perfect storm.

I didn't coin the expression, but I've heard it murmured plenty of times where I'm concerned. Let's just say I don't pine for female affection.

Not any night of the week.

Am I an arrogant bastard? Sometimes, but if the ladies are looking for the ride of their life—both on and off my hog—you'd better believe that's what they get.

Under promise and over deliver. My personal credo.

Kiki, the woman currently sitting across the desk from me, used to be one of those women. We had a fun fling about a million years ago, before she shacked up with our chief of police, Drake Briggs.

"Please, Kiki. I'll make it up to you. Any way you prefer." Leaning back in the chair, I toss my booted legs on the desk, pinning her with my golden-green stare.

I'd never move in on my buddy's old lady. She knows it and I know it, but judging by the flush climbing Kiki's cheeks, I can still press her hot buttons. For this scenario, believe me, I'm pushing *all* of them.

"Don't give me that look, Ash. It only worked when we were sleeping together," Kiki scoffs, shooting me a crooked smirk. "If I bend the rules for you, I have to do it for everyone. Although, I have an idea that might work."

My ears perk up. Maybe Kiki will offer to speak to the Frost Witch on my behalf. After all, she claims Oriana is lovely.

To me, that's like calling a piranha friendly, but if she's willing to take one for the team, I'm sure as hell going to allow it.

"I'm listening."

Kiki's grin widens. "Now, I know this may be difficult for you, but what if you try being your normal, charming self? Take another stab at being neighborly. Who knows? Oriana Thorne might surprise even you."

"That's your big idea? Some help you are."

"Just try it. Don't go in there with a chip on your shoulder from some perceived grievance—"

"I didn't start this," I argue, letting my feet slide to the ground with a thud.

"Maybe not, but if you want to start the speakeasy project, you need to finish this first. Bottom line, I can't help you here. But I know you when you want something, Asher Hammond. You're unstoppable."

"Easy for you to say. You don't have to tangle with Oriana's dark side."

Kiki pulls her keys from her purse and walks toward the door. "Never thought I'd see the day when a tiny woman could scare a man like you."

She's fucking with me, but she also knows that poking at my masculine ego is the best way to coax me into gear.

"Aren't you funny?" Another loud groan escapes my chest as I push myself from the chair. "Nothing can melt that ice queen, but I want the speakeasy opened, and she's my only obstacle."

Everything hinges on my snarky neighbor's seal of approval.

Kiki seems certain it won't be difficult to get Oriana on board with my plans, but I know better.

I stand a better chance of convincing an orca that a seal isn't a delicacy.

"I GUESS IT WASN'T GOOD NEWS," BRADEN OBSERVES, glancing up from his latest client design when I trudge into his studio space.

"That's an understatement. Kiki says I'm screwed if I don't get Oriana's signature. No way around it."

"You knew that already, though."

"Still thought I might convince her to change her mind."

Braden shakes his head and snorts at my words. "I'm sure her husband would love to hear how you plan on doing that."

"Probably not worth the jail time."

"Definitely not."

Despite his ribbing, Braden, like Kiki, knows I don't eat

off another man's plate. I did that once, albeit unknowingly, and it haunts me to this day.

Some lines you don't cross.

Now, if Kiki had requested I bury Oriana Thorne under a newly poured foundation, I might have considered *that* proposition.

I'm kidding, of course, although it seems easy compared with my current mission.

My gaze tracks along the walls of Braden's studio, searching for an answer amongst the artwork and awards littering the walls.

Sadly, there is none to be found.

It's then I spy the violet coffee cup sitting on the workspace next to my younger brother. I'd recognize the branding anywhere—it's from One More Page.

Aka, Oriana Thorne's bookstore.

"You've got to be fucking kidding me." I snatch up the cup, sending my brother a withering glare. "Fraternizing with the enemy now?"

Braden sighs, tapping his stylus against his tablet. "Man, I know you don't like her, but the woman brews some seriously good coffee."

"She doesn't make it. The coffee pot does all the work. All her petulant ass does is pour some beans into a filter. What a talent."

Am I being petty? Damn right, but every mention of her riles me up. Now I have to listen to Braden sing her praises?

"What's wrong with our coffee?" I demand, my boot tapping out an erratic rhythm against the wood floor.

See? Totally riled up. Who needs caffeine when you've got pure, unadulterated loathing at your fingertips?

Braden yanks the cup from my grasp, downing a sip. "Where do I start? How about the fact that it's sludge? Besides, she has the Jamaican blend I like, and I can't get it anywhere else in Sparkwood."

"I'll make you a deal. I order you several kilos of your preferred coffee bean and you stay away from that woman."

My brother's face splits into a grin at my offer. "Ash, that woman has got you all hot and bothered."

"Not even close."

His brows raise, and I catch his smirk as he returns his attention to his drawing. "Never seen a woman elicit such a reaction from you."

"That's because I like most women."

"You want me to speak to Oriana? I might have better luck, considering how much you detest her."

"I'm perfectly capable of holding a conversation with the woman."

"Sure about that?" He holds up his hands in a sign of surrender, but I note how the bastard is still biting back a grin. "I'm just saying, if you want her to agree, best not to go over there with guns blazing. *I* can manage that feat. Can *you?*"

Running a hand along my jaw, I catch sight of myself in the mirror on the far wall of the parlor. Braden is right—the woman *has* gotten under my skin. I'm a bundle of nerves every time I hear her name or see her pass by.

I can either defer to my brother and let him handle the situation, or I can take care of said situation myself.

Since I'm not one to run from my problems, that leaves me one option.

Oriana and I will have a come to Jesus meeting. By the

end, we'll both either be dead or in agreement. To be honest, it's anyone's guess which way this battle will go.

"Well?" Braden presses, his hazel eyes locked on me.

"I appreciate your offer, but I need to do this. Tomorrow night, once Black Lotus closes, I'll have a little chat with her."

"That way no one can hear your screams?" He's joking. At least, I hope it doesn't come to that, or Ms. Tight Ass and I will *both* be paying a noise ordinance fine.

I grab a bottle of water from the fridge before shooting Braden another scowl. "Look at you—a comedian."

"Hardly, although I think Oriana will surprise you."

"Doubtful. Kiki claims all I need to do is toss a little charm Oriana's way and it will all work out in the end."

"Sounds simple."

If only that were the case, but I'm smart enough to realize nothing could be further from the truth.

"Not with that woman, it isn't."

Chapter 2

Between a Date and a Hard Place

Ash

Turns out, there is a major kink in my plan and that kink is in the form of a beautiful woman.

No, I'm not referring to Oriana Thorne.

I mean, my lady for the evening, a prearranged good time that totally slipped my mind. At least, until she sashays through the door of Black Lotus and makes a beeline for my office.

"You ready to go, Ash?"

I glance up from my laptop, my mind blanking at her question.

She rests a hand on her hip, her lower lip pushing out in a pout. "Don't tell me you forgot. I spent hours getting ready for our date."

First, it's *not* a date, but I rarely correct women on the terminology. She knows it's a casual hangout because that is the *only* type of dating I do. Second, I'm an asshole and not for the first reason.

Despite my packed schedule, I never forget a meetup,

especially when they end up with a gorgeous woman naked in my arms.

And this woman is a looker and a half. She's poured herself into a pair of tight leather pants and a top that barely covers her enormous tits, leaving no curve to the imagination and no doubt about her plans for extracurricular activities.

But this lovely woman also conflicts with my primary plan for the evening—my chat with Oriana Thorne.

"You're not canceling, are you?" She shifts her weight from one heel to the other, apprehension wafting off her voice.

One thing I never do is disappoint a woman. Some men get off on shattering a woman's confidence. I'm not one of them.

Women have no clue how spectacular they are, in every sense of the word.

I don't believe in love, but I sure as hell believe in worshipping a woman's attributes.

So, I slide on a reassuring smile as my gaze moves along her figure. "Of course I'm not canceling, Lydia. Just have a few things to finish up. Shouldn't take more than fifteen minutes. Do you mind sticking around?"

"For you? No problem. Do you like my outfit?" Lydia pivots, offering me a glimpse of her ample assets.

"I do."

Hey, I'm not lying, although I wonder why women try so hard to be sexy when they're already inherently sensual creatures. They don't require all the spackle they slather on their faces or the surgeries to repair perceived shortcomings.

But when they feel beautiful, they also feel free. And

freedom is so much damn fun. When I entertain women, the release of all inhibitions is my goal.

Since I don't want to disappoint Lydia, it appears any discussion about tenancy rights with my pain-in-the-ass neighbor will have to wait for another night.

Yet another setback in my speakeasy quest.

Lydia motions toward the entrance of Black Lotus. "Take your time. I'll be in the bookstore next door. Come find me when you're finished."

Fuck me.

I *never* set foot in One More Page. Even if zombies were chasing my happy ass, I'd chance it on the outside, rather than darken Oriana Thorne's door.

She returns the favor by staying far away from Black Lotus.

Trust me, that's the *only* thing the Ice Queen and I agree on.

My hope is that when I venture into Oriana's shop to chat with her about our shared basement space, she'll understand the gravity of my situation just by my very presence in her store.

Then, once we finish with our tête-à-tête, we'll return to our normally scheduled avoidance.

It was a solid plan too until Lydia changed the play by going next door to shop behind enemy lines.

If I want to get laid tonight, and I'm pretty damn sure my lady friend has the same idea, I can't holler for her from the shared hallway like an auctioneer.

Even I have more tact than that.

I'll walk in, grab Lydia, and leave. Simple.

Twenty minutes later, I stroll into One More Page, half

expecting a bomb to go off the second my boots hit the hardwood floor.

Maybe I'll get lucky, and Lydia will be done and raring to go.

But I release a strangled grunt when I fix my eyes on her leather clad ass. Not only is she still browsing, but she's also chatting with the devil herself.

Oriana Thorne.

"Fucking hell," I mutter, dragging a hand through my hair.

So much for best laid plans. Here goes nothing.

I shove my hands into my jean pockets and walk over to the corner reading nook where the two ladies sit ensconced, a coffee-table book open between them.

"Ready to go?" I ask, careful to maintain a neutral tone in my voice.

Both women glance up. A smile cuts across one face. A dour frown crosses the other.

Bet you can figure out which is which.

"You finally made it," Lydia says, reaching up to thread her fingers through my belt loop. "Oriana and I were talking about France."

Personally, I don't care what they were discussing. I just want to leave. Now.

I nod, careful to avoid the petite bookshop owner's glare, which is currently cutting holes into me. "Is that right?"

"Have you been to France, Ash?" Lydia inquires, oblivious to the imaginary daggers being pitched my way by Oriana.

"Can't say that I have."

"We should go one day. Wouldn't that be fun?"

At this point, I'd agree to visit Mars with the woman, so long as it gets her ass moving from the store.

Lydia turns to Oriana, a smile splitting her face. "Your store is magical. You're a most amazing addition to Sparkwood."

In my defense, I didn't mean for the scoff to fly out of my mouth. It just happened.

Oriana's expression shifts into overdrive as she turns the full force of her glare on me. "You have something to add, Mr. Hammond?"

So many things, Ms. Thorne. How much time do you have?

I bite back the smirk, but it's no use. "Nope."

Oriana stands up and walks toward me until she's less than a foot from my side. Then she pushes her glasses up the bridge of her nose, plants her hands on her hips, and glowers up at me.

God, you do not play fair. I pray my poker face kicks in, because Oriana's stern pose is not garnering the reaction she hopes for.

Sorry to break it to you, sweetheart, but you're hardly intimidating.

In truth, if she wasn't such a frosty bitch, her aggressive stance would be wickedly adorable right now—like an angry Chihuahua taking on a Rottweiler. Thankfully, I manage to keep *that* thought safely within the confines of my brain.

"Really, because your expression says otherwise." Oriana clicks her tongue against her teeth, her eyes never wavering from my face.

Daring me to say what I'm thinking out loud.

I can do one of two things: engage with her anger or tease her. I'm pretty sure which one will piss her off more, and of course, that's the option I choose.

No, it's not the wiser move, but one might say Oriana brings it out of me.

I cross my arms over my chest and look down at her, a wide grin splitting my face. "You sure are feisty for someone so small."

Lydia giggles at my comment, but Oriana doesn't laugh. In fact, I bet money she's plotting my murder. No joke. If looks could kill, I'd be buried several feet under right now.

Should I have kept my mouth shut? Probably.

Was it worth it to watch the fire ignite in her eyes? Absolutely.

I gear up for round two, but my petite adversary has a different idea.

Oriana averts her eyes as she grabs the books off the coffee table, shaking her head in disgust. "So typical. Lydia, it was lovely meeting you. And *you*"—she hisses, once again pinning me with her gaze—"may you have the day you deserve."

She storms away, toward a rickety ladder perched against one of the floor-to-ceiling bookshelves.

Lydia's eyes widen as she watches Oriana's departure. "What was that about?"

"Nothing," I mutter, feeling a twinge of guilt kick in at Oriana's reaction. Although, it's not my fault the woman lacks a sense of humor.

"Are you two …" Lydia's voice trails off as she gestures between Oriana and me.

"Are we what?"

"Sleeping together? Did I step on some toes by coming over here?"

My brows fly up at her intimation. "Me and her? What in the world would give you that idea?"

Lydia shrugs and grabs her purse. "Something about the way you two are together. Your energy."

"We spend a whole lot of it hating one another."

"Oh, I get it. You *used* to sleep together."

What is with this crazy conversation train?

Shaking my head, I gently steer Lydia toward the exit. "We've never done anything together, except argue and plot ways to avoid each other. Good enough answer for you?"

Lydia pauses before falling into step with me. "Sure. Guess I read it wrong."

You sure did, sweetheart.

One thing is for certain: I can't get out of here fast enough.

But luck is not on my side tonight.

As we stroll past the worn ladder, a gasp sounds above us, only seconds before one of the hardcover books tumbles to the ground with a thud.

Glares from Oriana are one thing, but now she's throwing crap at me?

After dodging the falling book, I scowl up at the Oriana, gearing up to toss a heated retort in her direction.

But the words die in my throat.

The rickety ladder is on its last legs—literally.

The rung on which Oriana stands is cracked, and with every passing second, her weight, slight though it may be, is testing its last vestiges of strength.

But it's the look on Oriana's face that erases the anger from my brain. Her eyes are wide and frantic, her hands wrapped around the sides of the ladder in a death grip.

Grabbing the ladder to steady it, I look up at her. "Come on down. I've got the ladder."

A frown creases her brow, but she remains rooted to the spot. "Wouldn't you rather knock it out from under me and finish the job?"

I swear to God, this woman is jumping on my last nerve.

"Sure, which explains why I'm holding it right now. Look, I've got places to be, so if you'd hurry and get your ass down here, I'd appreciate it."

But she doesn't move. Oriana's expression wavers between fear and frustration, no doubt weighing her options: a fall on her head from eight feet in the air or allowing me, the detestable inked hoodlum, to function as her knight in shining armor.

"I'm going to count to three, and then you're on your own. One, two—"

"Sorry," she mumbles, her foot searching out the rung below her. "I'm terrified of heights."

"Then why are you on the ladder?"

Some women make no sense.

"Good question," she whispers, another whimper escaping her throat when her foot slips.

Enough of this nonsense.

I shrug off my jacket and hand it to Lydia before climbing the six rungs to reach Oriana, all the while praying the damn ladder holds us both.

A trip to the emergency department with this woman is not on my agenda for the evening.

"What are you doing?" Oriana asks, shooting me a confused look over one shoulder.

"Getting you down. Turn around."

"I can't."

"Yes, you can. Release your right hand and grab my arm. Then turn yourself slowly and hold on to me."

Oriana hesitates, and I wonder if she's prepping for another argument. Instead, she releases a deep sigh and abides my request, her hands gripping the fabric of my shirt in a stranglehold.

"Now, wrap your arms around my neck and your legs around my waist. I'll do the hard work. You just hold on to me."

"You promise you won't drop me?"

Maybe it's the blatant fear in her face or the timidity in her voice. For the first time, I see the human side of Oriana Thorne.

"Hey," I murmur in a voice normally reserved for the bedroom. "I would never drop you. Believe that."

She peeks at the ground and releases another whimper before wrapping herself around me.

I slide my hand under her ass to hold her steady and take a careful step down. So far, so good.

But when Oriana buries her face in my neck, my entire world shifts on its axis.

My mind blanks as her scent assails my nostrils.

I don't know what the hell she's wearing, but it's intoxicating. Warm and sweet, with an undercurrent of sandalwood and jasmine, all mixing to wreak havoc on my senses.

Or maybe it's just her. The woman smells like heaven, and I fight the urge to drag my tongue along her ivory skin. Does she taste this delicious, too?

My blood pounds in my ears, but I can't wrap my head around any thought but her. I'm hyperaware of every inch of Oriana's form pressed to mine, and how damn *good* she feels in my arms.

Fuck Ash, get it together.

"Are you two okay up there? Do I need to grab one of the guys next door?" Lydia's voice breaks into the moment and I shake my head to clear it.

How long was I perched on this ladder with this woman clinging to me?

That's it. Oriana Thorne is a damn siren—a beautiful but deadly creature who seduces a man before dragging him to a watery grave. Or in this case, a crash to the floor below.

"We're fine. Just another loose rung." I duck my head toward Oriana's face, still burrowed against me. "Are you ready?"

Oriana lifts her head, her dark eyes wide behind her glasses. She bites her lip and glances at the floor. "I'm ready. You sure I'm not too heavy?"

"Not even a little bit."

With careful, measured steps, I descend the ladder, her siren scent messing with me the entire time.

Much more of this, and I won't be accountable for my actions.

But Oriana doesn't release her grip on me, even though we're safely on solid ground. She clutches at me as though terrified the floor might suddenly give way beneath us.

"We're off the ladder," I whisper, my hand offering a reassuring stroke along her spine. "You're okay."

And she *is* fine. I'm the one who isn't okay.

Her breath warms my neck, her lips hovering so close to my skin that I can almost feel them.

Now, I'm nursing *another* problem and need to put some distance between us immediately.

"Thank you." Her voice is soft and her lower lip wobbles as she chances a glance in my direction.

Fuck, Oriana has a beautiful mouth. Then again, aren't sirens notoriously appealing, right before they drag you to your death?

"Can we go now? I really need that drink." Lydia clears her throat, her foot tapping the floor as she shoots darts in our direction.

Easy, sweetheart. You'll get your turn.

But unless Lydia's angling for a threesome, I need to deal with the petite woman in my arms—a woman who seems in no hurry to escape.

Looks like the Ice Queen has a heart, after all. Or at least a healthy libido.

I shoot Oriana my trademark smirk. "Darling, I know you like being in my arms, but my date is waiting."

Oriana's gaze clears as though she was part of the same trancelike state as me. Shaking her head, she scrambles off me, gifting me with a flash of her stomach before yanking her shirt down. "Right. Sorry about that."

Her words say one thing, but her gestures and the flush climbing her cheeks say another.

Maybe I'm a bastard, but I love the idea that she felt it, too.

Whatever *it* was.

I take my coat from Lydia, shooting another cocky grin toward Oriana. "Not a problem. Happy to be of service, although you didn't have to fall off a ladder to get my attention. You could have just told me you wanted to be in my arms."

Oriana scoffs and shoves her glasses up her nose. "For a second there, I actually thought you were a nice guy. My mistake."

And once again, the boxing gloves are on.

I'm not sure why her caustic reply irks me so much, but there is no way I'll allow this woman the last word.

Seems she isn't done shooting zingers in my direction. "I'm shocked you didn't let me fall." Her voice is low as she picks at an imaginary thread on her blouse, her cheeks bright pink.

I glare at her as my heroic moment twists into frustration. "Trust me, I considered it. But then I remembered I have far more important places to be than waiting here for the ambulance."

"Enjoy your date, or whatever you call it," she snaps.

"You know, a thank you would be nice, or is that too tricky for a woman like you?"

She worries her lower lip with her teeth and shifts her weight. "Thank you."

"Wow. That was almost believable. Don't worry, sunshine. Next time, I'll make sure to walk away first."

I storm toward the door, acutely aware of my date watching our heated exchange. "Let's go."

"You sure?" My date nods toward Oriana, who is gathering up the few books that fell off the shelf during our tangle up. "Let me guess. She's not happy you're going out with me."

"Why would she care? We hate each other, remember?"

"Is that what you call it?"

"Despise, loathe. Those are acceptable terms, too."

She nods, unconvinced. "Hmm."

"What?"

"Didn't look that way from here."

"What was I supposed to do? Let her fall on her head? Despite what *she* thinks, I'm not a bastard."

My date turns and pushes open the bookstore door, strolling a few steps ahead, her ample assets swaying in front of me. "That's not what *she* thinks either. It's what she wants you to think."

I shake my head and follow her to my bike, handing her the spare helmet. "Come on, let's focus on our night."

IT CAN NEVER BE SIMPLE, CAN IT?

My idea to focus on Lydia isn't working, because I can't stop thinking about Oriana. As the evening drags on, Oriana's words and the look in her eyes keep playing over and over in my brain, gnawing at me.

By the time I finish my first drink, I know I have to end the night early.

I set my glass down and look over at my date. "I'm sorry, but I need to cut this short. There's something I need to take care of."

She gives me a knowing look, a mix of disappointment and sarcasm. "Let me guess, a bookstore emergency? I hope you two figure out whatever unresolved issues you have."

"It's not like that. It's business."

"Asher Hammond, isn't everything in your world?" Lydia shakes her head and finishes her drink. "Let's go. Why delay the inevitable?"

Lydia is pissed, and rightfully so, but it doesn't matter.

Will I pass up on a night of guaranteed sex to ensure I have a signed lease for my speakeasy?

Absolutely.

Besides, I can make it up to my date another night when I prove to her it really *is* just business.

I ride back to the parking lot, offering Lydia a chaste kiss before watching her drive out of view.

Then I turn my focus to the dimly lit interior of One More Page. The store is closed, but Oriana's truck is still in the lot.

Perfect.

Chapter 3

The Heart of the Grudge

Ori

"That's it. The world is coming to an end. That's the only explanation I can figure for what I witnessed earlier today."

I quirk a brow at my coworker, Mina, as she deposits a stack of books next to me on the counter. "What are you talking about?"

"Asher Hammond was in One More Page. Never thought I'd see the day."

I roll my eyes and grab the top book on the pile, flipping through the pages. "When did we get this in? Did you order it?"

Mina lowers the book in my hands before sending me a knowing smirk. "Don't change the subject."

"Why would I want to discuss a subject as undesirable as Asher Hammond?"

Mina bites her lip, but a small giggle escapes her mouth. "Maybe because he climbed up that deathtrap of a ladder to rescue you."

Well, fuck. I was hoping Mina missed that slice of the evening.

"He said it was a one-time deal. Next time, he'd watch me fall."

Her eyes widen at my words. "He said that? Really?"

"Right hand to God," I reply.

Look, I won't admit it to Mina, but I'm grateful Asher was there. Grateful and mortified, in equal measure. No doubt he's reveling in the idea that he now has something to lord over me.

As if the man needs more fodder for his portfolio on hating me.

He's got volumes on that subject.

Mina rests her hand on my arm, giving it a gentle squeeze. "He wouldn't. He'd save you every time."

A nice thought. Total crap, but I'll give the woman points for trying.

My bet is Asher only saved *me* to save face in front of his fuck buddy. If it had only been the two of us in the store, he would have left me dangling in midair, tossing a chuckle up for good measure as he walked past.

I exhale sharply, eager to shift the conversation to something less aggravating. "There won't be any need to save me again. That ladder is heading to the dumpster first thing in the morning."

"He smells good, though, doesn't he?"

"I have no idea," I reply through gritted teeth.

Another lie, considering I spent a few minutes clinging to him like a terrified kitten stuck in a tree.

And to answer Mina's question, Asher smells amazing. He also feels amazing, with biceps as big around as my head.

But of course, none of that matters, because one trait stands out above *all* the others: he's an egotistical jackass.

Mina has some nerve, insinuating I actually enjoyed my time in Asher Hammond's arms.

My only hope is a sudden attack of amnesia so that *I* might forget the entire event.

Forget the snarky look in his eyes and the cruel curl of his lip when he put me in my place—yet again.

The worst part of this entire situation? I'm a likable person, and the people of Sparkwood agree. Hell, even his date and I got along, although I question her taste in men.

But to Asher Hammond, I'm the Ice Queen. Yep, that's my nickname, courtesy of the county's biggest player. How do I know this little tidbit? It's a small town, and people talk. Let's just say it only made me hate him more once I learned his moniker for me.

"I'll never understand what women see in him," I mutter.

"You don't? Seriously, you're not blind," Mina teases, nodding toward the coffee bar. "Come on, let me make you a cup."

I glance out the window at the falling darkness. "It's after six. I'll be up all night."

"We'll do decaf then."

Mina seems determined to fix us a hot beverage, but as I slide onto a stool at the far end of the bar, I realize it's not due to a hankering for caffeine.

From her position behind the coffee bar, she has a clear view into Black Lotus's reception area, easily visible across our shared hallway.

And a certain tattoo artist just so happens to be

lounging there, his long legs casually propped up on a table as he chats with a customer.

"I should have known you had an ulterior motive behind this spur-of-the-moment coffee fix," I remark, biting back a grin. "Front-row seat for Braden Hammond, huh?"

Mina straightens her stance and releases a noisy breath. "Not at all. I didn't know he was sitting there. Total coincidence."

Seems I'm not the only one spouting falsehoods tonight. "Uh-huh."

When Mina catches my quirked brow, she turns away, her face flushing as she hurriedly busies herself with frothing the milk. "Fine. Braden Hammond is hot, okay? Sue me."

I help myself to a chocolate chip cookie from the case. "Knew it. Falling for the enemy. A traitor in my midst."

"He stopped in here this morning." She holds up her hands as if warding off any further argument from me. "I know you hate his brother, but Braden is really sweet."

"Braden *is* nice." With a shrug, I turn my attention to the laminated menu, flicking at one corner. "And if Asher were more like his brother, he and I wouldn't have any issues. But he's not, and we do."

"You sure hate him."

"For your information, I don't *hate* Asher. The man isn't worth that level of energy."

But Mina knows me too well to believe that rigmarole. "Right. That's why you toss death stares at him every time he dares to pass our window."

The truth? I can't stand Asher Hammond. He's an egotistical oaf, a typical alpha male who will never admit that he or his tatted-up buddies could *ever* be in the wrong.

Still, what's the point of discussing his arrogant ways? It's not like the man is capable of change. Hell, he isn't even capable of an apology.

And because he doesn't deem me worthy of an apology, I hardly feel the need to heap on gratitude for his 'heroic' efforts earlier today.

I'll admit that I'm glad Ash saved my terrified ass from the broken ladder. It would have been a nasty fall, and instead of drinking coffee, I'd be at the hospital getting X-rays of my skull.

And for those few moments in his arms, I felt safe. Safer than I'd ever known possible, like the entire world could have ended and somehow, he would have shielded me from the blow.

Obviously, a ridiculous notion concocted by my overly romanticized brain, considering Asher Hammond would no doubt take great pleasure in pitching my ass off any of the pine covered peaks surrounding Sparkwood.

But the worst part was the way his demeanor changed on a dime when Lydia spoke. The softness in his voice and eyes disappeared, replaced by his ever present—and always annoying—smirk. A reminder that he's God's gift to women and I'm a damn fool if I don't fall in line with that mentality.

Then, in true Asher Hammond fashion, he cut me down to size.

I hate how he makes me feel that level of animosity. Hate that he makes me feel anything at all.

Still, I'm happy he was in the store when the ladder rung cracked, although I'd rather toss my ass to the ground repeatedly than admit that fact aloud.

I pull off my glasses, cleaning the lens with my shirt

hem as I fight to maintain a neutral expression. "Let's put it this way. Despite the events of today, he's still not on my Christmas card list, although I might cave and buy him a lump of coal."

Mina busies herself making coffee, but judging by the side-eye she shoots at me, she's far from done with this conversation. She's desperate to understand the root of the animosity between the owner of Black Lotus and me, but despite her repeated digging, I've never said a word.

Why bring up such an undesirable topic?

Asher and I can't stand the sight of one another.

It's an intense, mutual emotion.

End of story.

Mina slides a mug of coffee to me, and I accept with a smile. "Best brew in town."

"Spill it, Ori. What the hell happened between you and Asher? Did you sleep with him, or something?"

I sputter my drink at her unexpected inquiry. "I most certainly did not."

"Most of the town loves the man."

"Probably because most of the town has slept with him."

Hey, I'm not lying. In the six months since I moved to Sparkwood, Asher Hammond's name has danced on the tips of countless tongues like a favorite treat.

Apparently, his sexual prowess is second to none, although he never keeps company with any woman for long. I've lost count of the number of beautiful women who hop on the back of his Harley at closing time, speeding away into the dark.

I've also never seen the same woman twice.

One would think *that* part of his reputation would be as

noteworthy as the size of his cock, but it seems to be a non-issue.

Guess there's no accounting for taste.

Mina snaps her fingers, a sly grin splitting her face. "See? That's the problem. You two need to screw and release all this pent-up aggression."

"Hard pass. Besides, he's got his flavor of the night to do that for him."

"Is someone jealous?"

I snort out a laugh. "Seriously? Not even close."

"You don't think he's hot?"

Swinging my gaze to Mina, I peer at her over the top of my glasses. "Beauty is more than skin deep."

"True, but Asher Hammond is damn fine."

With a scoff, I swig down more coffee, desperate to find another conversation path. I'd rather discuss boils on the butt of an aardvark than the comely owner of Black Lotus tattoo.

"Ori, what the hell did he do to you?"

Huffing out a sigh, I realize my young friend has no intention of letting this matter drop. I get it. Since my initial meeting with Asher, relations between the two shops have been tenser than an early morning duel, and it's trickling down to the rest of the staff.

My employees live in a battle zone, with no idea what precipitated the war.

"Fine, I'll tell you, but don't say I didn't warn you."

Mina leans her elbows on the bar. "Duly noted."

"Right after opening One More Page, I hosted a poetry reading. I specifically chose a day when Black Lotus closed early, because I know things can get loud over there, particularly after dark. A moot point, since music blasted from next door, along with a constant stream of obscenities and sexually offensive declarations. We couldn't hear a word the poet said over the din, even with a microphone."

"Damn."

"Still, I'm the new girl in town, right? Must tread lightly. I walked next door and asked them to keep it down. I even brought coffee and baked goods as a peace offering, but the guy who answered the door told me to shove my goodies up my ass. He declared he could—and *would*—do whatever he damn well pleased because he had Asher's permission. When I dared argue the fact, he made a snide comment about Asher warning him about me being a prissy bitch, and that if I didn't keep my mouth shut, Asher would personally make me sorry. Then he slammed the door in my face."

Mina's mouth drops open, her eyes as wide as the coffee mugs. "Holy shit. What an asshole. But wait a minute. You said it wasn't Asher spouting this crap, so why do you hate him?"

"Give me a minute. I'm getting to Asher's shining moment."

"Can't wait to hear it. Am I going to want to pour coffee over his head after this?"

"I know I do," I volley back. "After that night, I had two options: let it lie or have a chat with Asher. You know I don't back down, so I confronted Asher about it, and he acted like I was insane. Claimed the noise *couldn't* have come from Black Lotus because they were closed. He just stood there, his arms crossed over his chest, this smirk on his mouth, like he was enjoying every second of watching me squirm. That pissed me off worse than his buddy the night before. After realizing nothing would be rectified, I left and threatened to call the cops the next time they made that kind of racket."

"Seems fair," Mina states, sipping her coffee. "You were nicer than I would have been."

I hold up my hand, stopping her conversation midstream. "I haven't gotten to the best part yet. Asher Hammond followed me over here and bawled me out, right in front of my customers. Then he called me a prissy bitch, the same terminology used by his hooligan friend the night before. Seems everyone at Black Lotus felt the same way about me, and since I was the newbie, I was shit out of luck. Asher reminded me of that fact when he told me to call the police chief, who was one of *his* best friends. I know how small towns work, Mina, and my issues were falling on deaf ears." I click my tongue against my teeth, the distaste from my initial meeting with Asher still bitter in my mouth. "That was that."

"Well, I see why he isn't getting a Christmas card."

I lob my napkin at Mina's head, releasing a chuckle. "Don't you have some work to do? What am I paying you for?"

"Counseling, apparently. Letting you release all your anger about the big, mean tattoo artist residing next door."

"Trust me, I've got plenty more where that came from."

Chapter 4

One More Page, One Last Nerve

Ori

Mina pokes her head into my office an hour later, jerking her thumb toward the door. "The shop is closed up, and I'm heading out."

I nod in her general direction, but I'm more focused on our accounting figures for the last quarter. One More Page is doing better than original estimates, and the numbers keep growing.

See? Sometimes busting your ass pays off.

"Ori, are you listening?"

"Yes, but I'm sticking around for a while. I want to get a jump on decorating the window for the Christmas season."

"Do you need me to stay?"

Darling Mina. She's dogged in her determination to help others, although most people only focus on her outward beauty. Trust me, she's stunning, but that's the least wonderful aspect of the woman.

No doubt that's part of why she's so giving and helpful. I've overheard a few women in town gossiping about her behind her back—nasty, catty bitches who can't imagine that a woman who looks like a living Barbie could have a good heart.

Likely explains why she spends most evenings alone. A real shame, and one day, a real man will realize what a prize she is, whisk in, and scoop her up.

"Get out of here, Mina. I'll see you tomorrow."

"Stay off the damn ladder. Promise me."

"No problem. The easiest deal in history. Now go."

With a mock salute, she closes my office door, leaving me to my own devices.

I love the solitude. There's something so peaceful about walking around the store and realizing that every book, mug, bag, and muffin—are mine.

I never imagined I'd wind up living in a tiny town in upstate New York. Then again, I never figured I'd be single at thirty-nine, either.

In every group of friends, there is one diehard romantic. In my group, that was me. I love the idea of love—the bigger, the better. My ideals make me the perfect bridesmaid, and trust me, I've stood up next to more than a dozen friends as they exchanged vows.

I've also sat on the couch holding tissues and chocolate, consoling half those women when their marriages went south.

So, while I adore the concept of happily ever after, more often than not, my all-encompassing view of the L word keeps me sidelined.

I'm not interested in doing something halfway. I want it all—the passion, the excitement, the earth-shattering love.

That's a big part of the reason I'm single.

Men ask me out all the time, but if he doesn't awaken something inside me, he's not worth the bother.

An added issue is most men my age fall into two categories: either they have already walked the marriage path and have no interest in pursuing it again, or they're like Asher Hammond—content to bed a different woman every night of the week.

So, instead of snuggling up to a handsome man tonight, I'll focus on making Christmas dreams come true for Sparkwood. One More Page has a prime spot on Main Street, and the locals love browsing the holiday window displays.

Browsing often turns to buying, and my quarterly receipts prove that the residents of Sparkwood need One More Page in their lives.

All except for the men at Black Lotus. But to be fair, I'm riding on the assumption they even know how to read.

Look, it has zero to do with their appearance or their sexual prowess.

I don't discriminate based on the amount of ink on someone's skin or the number of lovers they take. Your body—do what you want with it. I do, however, harbor an intense dislike for assholes and Asher Hammond holds the crown in that category.

I scrub my face, grunting as I force the memory of Asher holding me out of my mind. He's likely on his second round with Lydia by now, or maybe his third, depending on how much wooing she requires.

Either way, he doesn't deserve another thought.

Time to focus on the task at hand.

I remove the fall-themed items currently decorating the window and schlep them to the top of the basement stairs.

I love that there is storage space under the shop, even if I am sharing said area with Black Lotus Tattoo. It's an odd set-up, but according to the building's owner, Kiki, it's standard in this area.

The basement access lies through a nondescript door at the end of a jointly shared hallway. Beyond that area, Black Lotus and One More Page are totally separate, with our own meters and internet access.

I can only imagine if we had to share that, too.

A quick glimpse through the windows of Black Lotus reveals the darkened interior, which is yet another bonus. If their shop is closed, there is zero chance of a run-in with any of the employees.

Trust me, one interaction per day with Asher is *more* than enough.

To be fair, Braden and Zane seem lovely, although I rarely see them. When I do, they smile and wave before going about their business.

Asher Hammond is the exception to the rule.

I hate when people dislike me, especially when I have done nothing to deserve said treatment.

But there isn't a chance in hell I'll let Asher insult me and get away with it, even if he did carry my ass off that suicide mission of a ladder earlier.

And Mina would love for me to mend fences with the resident tattoo god, even if getting to know his brother better is her ulterior motive.

Not happening, lovely.

Flipping on the light, I carry the boxes downstairs. By the third trip, I've broken a sweat and am seriously reconsidering my plans for Christmas window dressing. On a positive note, I won't need the gym tonight.

My front window stands bare with a last load of decor

ready to return to hibernation. I perch the pumpkins on top of the box and tuck the last scarecrow under my arm. Then, with the grace of a drunken elk, I fumble down the stairs.

When a stray pumpkin slips from my grasp and rolls across the dimly lit basement, I decide to throw in the towel.

That's enough for tonight.

I'll awaken Santa from his slumber in the morning.

Time for a bubble bath and a glass of wine. Yes, that will do nicely.

I snatch the pumpkin from its hiding place under a table, brushing away a stray cobweb.

Funny, but I've never looked at the space from this angle before. Kiki mentioned when I first signed the lease that this was a speakeasy during Prohibition, and celebrities from all over the area partied until the wee hours of the night.

Didn't hurt that the police chief at the time was a regular, or so goes the story.

Even though it's a bit on the dingy side now, I see the potential in the space. There is history in these walls and stories just waiting to be told. In the darkened corners, I can almost see the outlines of her former patrons, leaning against the brick walls, gin in hand, as jazz music ebbs through the air.

Even the original oak bar still stands along one side, now coated in a fine layer of dust.

"The things you've seen," I murmur aloud, tracing my fingertips along the bar's brass inlay. "And the secrets you keep."

She needs work, but it's a magnificent spot for a bar,

and it would be a huge draw in Sparkwood. Locals here love their history and their spirits—liquid and otherwise.

There have been rumblings in town about renovating the basement and returning her to her old glory. Word on the street is that Asher Hammond wants to take the reins on that project.

Not that he's said a word to me.

No surprise there.

However, if he hopes to move forward, he must ensure I'm on board with the idea.

After all, that's the agreement in the original lease. When he showed up in my store earlier today, I assumed that was the reason, but instead of breaking bread and laying to rest our past grievances, he saved my ass and then played on my last nerve.

Interesting negotiation style, to be sure.

Will I grant him use of the space?

Maybe. Maybe not. I have no intention of making it easy for the man. He's going to have to—insert a gasp of shock and awe—be nice to me and humble himself enough to say he's sorry for treating me shabbily.

Then, and only then, I might consider his request.

Until that happens, he can kiss my ass.

Petty? Perhaps, but the bastard has it coming.

I carry the pumpkin to the back corner of the basement and safely stow the decorations on the shelves.

Time to get out of here. That glass of wine sounds better with every passing second.

A creaking sounds from the top of the stairs, startling me.

"This is what you get when you talk to ghosts, Ori," I mumble to myself with a chuckle.

Old buildings make all sorts of noises. The chance of an actual haunting is slim to none.

But then I hear footfalls on the stairs.

And that I'm not imagining.

My heart races in my chest as I realize, quite foolishly, that I never verified if Mina did indeed lock the door to One More Page.

"Crap. I'm not in the mood to die tonight."

Sparkwood is a safe town, but that doesn't mean it's without incident.

Just last week, the liquor store got robbed at gunpoint. Granted, it's more of a mark than a bookstore, but that doesn't mean someone hasn't been watching.

Waiting for the right moment.

Glancing around the dim space, I spy my only possible weapon—a push broom. "If this is my lone defense, I'm screwed."

The footsteps move closer, no doubt drawn to the light leeching from the corner. I grip the broom tighter, ready to greet whoever they belong to, while praying they're only a figment of my sleep-deprived imagination.

Or maybe it *is* a ghost, which would be a welcome reprieve at this point.

It's then I hear another sound—the upstairs door swinging shut.

A door that locks from the outside.

A door I'm certain I *didn't* unlock before I wedged it open.

Stupid, stupid, *stupid* woman.

And then I hear a deep male voice drawl, "I know you're down here. Might as well come out."

Chapter 5

Truth, Consequences, and Whiskey

Ori

The sheen of fear gives way to aggravation as I recognize the burly voice.

Asher Hammond.

With a grunt, I step from my hiding spot, still clinging to the broom. "What do you want?"

"Hello is a customary greeting."

"Why would I say hello to you?"

He shrugs. "Because it's polite? Granted, you don't like saying thank you, either, so I shouldn't be surprised."

"You want me to be polite to *you*? As I recall, you informed me that your initial impulse was to let me fall off the ladder."

Ash offers another shrug, the corners of his mouth turning up. No doubt he's picturing the scene in his head and relishing every second. "But I didn't, did I? And *I* recall you were all too happy to cling to me."

"As opposed to what? Cracking my skull open? What an option, Asher."

"I know which option you chose."

47

This. Fucking. Guy.

A growl rises from my chest, which only serves to amuse him further.

And then he spots my 'weapon.'

No way he's going to let this one slip by unmentioned.

Asher crosses his arms over his chest, a smirk coloring his face. It's the same pose from six months earlier. So glad the man still enjoys making me nuts. "What's the broom for?"

"Although you likely have a harem of women to perform these rudimentary chores, it's used for sweeping."

He moves closer, and I back away.

Now his expression borders on a sneer. "But you're not sweeping, are you? I think that's your weapon, sad as it may be. What's the matter? Are you scared?"

No way will I give the bastard the satisfaction of knowing he startled me. Instead, I rise to my full height—still more than a foot shorter than the man—and shoot off a glare. "Of you? Not a chance. Aggravated. Annoyed as hell. Perturbed. Those are far more accurate terms for describing how I feel about you."

A few seconds tick by, both of us standing our ground, our eyes locked on the other in a fiery battle of wills.

I break first, but only because I *really* need that glass of wine now. "Why are you down here?"

"It's my basement, too."

"Let me guess. You have a secret sex dungeon down here." And no doubt, Lydia is waiting in the wings, desperate for me to vacate the premises.

Trust me, Lydia, we're on the same page.

"Why? Are you interested?" Asher runs his hand over his bearded jaw, his movements slow and purposeful, drawing all my attention to his mouth—an action that doesn't go unnoticed. His lips quirk into a barely there smile, knowing damn well the effect he's having on me, even if I'd sooner die a fiery death than admit it.

"Not in the slightest." I shift my weight and avert my gaze to a distant point, determined to maintain an even keel.

I will not allow this ogre to upset me.

Asher shoves his hands into his pockets and rocks back on his heels. "Trust me, sweetheart. Your frigid ass could use it."

So much for remaining even keeled.

"Fuck you, Asher." I spit the words out, an enraged huff escaping my lips. Not my most original comeback, but I worry that using words too big might only confuse the Neanderthal.

He chuckles, a low, gravelly sound rising from his chest. "No thanks. As much as you'd love it, you're not my type."

I clench my teeth, wondering why his caustic comment stings. Of course, I'm not his type. I don't *want* to be his type.

"Coming from you, that's a compliment. Guess I'm special, since you've fucked everyone else in town."

Asher throws his head back, a dark laugh biting through his words. "Now you're jealous."

God, what I'd give to swing a frying pan at his head right now. That would wipe the smirk off his face.

"What does any woman see in you?" I grit my teeth as the rage bubbles through me.

He leans against the basement wall, that cocky grin playing across his face. I've seen it a hundred times before, but he's never aimed it in my direction. "Same thing you do, sweetheart."

Screw this crap. I just want to get out of here, go home and have a stiff drink. Forget the wine. My bottle of tequila is seeing some action tonight.

I shove past him and stomp up the stairs, hoping against all odds that, somehow, the door remains unlocked.

With a jiggle of the handle, my worst fears are confirmed.

It's not.

I pivot on the step. "You have a key to this door?"

Asher moves to the bottom of the stairs, peering up at me. "I do, but it's in Black Lotus."

Strike one.

I reach for my mobile phone, groaning when I realize I left it in the bookstore. "Please tell me you have your phone."

He shakes his head, but I see the amusement dancing across his face. So glad he's having a good time. Bully for him.

"How do you not have your phone?" I demand.

"You don't have yours."

Absolutely not. The man cannot use logic against me. That simply won't work.

Snapping my fingers, I earn an aggravated look from the tatted behemoth. "Thank God for Lydia, right? She'll figure out you're missing and come find you. Problem solved."

"She's home."

Fucking hell.

"Home? What is she doing there? I thought you two had a date—or whatever it is you call it. Your night was just getting started." I lower my voice in a poor imitation of Asher's, much to his growing amusement.

"Ended early."

I should let his comment lie and focus on my escape, but Asher fucking Hammond has trampled my ego one too many times. Screw decorum. "Oh, you finished that quickly, huh? How sad … for Lydia."

"You wish," Asher mutters, but I hear him whisper a curse under his breath.

Now, it's *my* turn to toss a haughty laugh his way. "Not if you were the last man on earth."

His gaze catches mine, and I see something flicker in their depths. Maybe I'm getting to him or maybe he's about to snap and end me. It's a toss up at this point.

But he drags a hand through his dark hair and clicks his tongue against his teeth. "We'll see about that, won't we?"

Much more of this torture and I'll pitch myself down the stairs. How would Mr. Wonderful talk his way out of that mess?

Opting for safety, I throw up my hands and flop down on the top step. "So, now what? We're stuck down here?"

Asher places one booted leg on the bottom step as a grin splits his face. "Looks that way. Looks like we're stuck together until tomorrow morning."

I rub my forehead, trying to will away the headache brewing in my brain. "Awesome. This is obviously penance for committing terrible crimes in a past life. Well, that settles it." Pushing myself to standing, I move past him, walking to the far corner of the basement and popping open a wooden box.

Asher tracks my movements from the other side of the

basement. "What are you doing now? Looking for a better weapon?"

"Nope. I can always shove that broomstick up your ass. That should shut you up for a while."

Asher snorts and shakes his head, which is *not* helping me manage my anger.

Turing to face him, I plant my hands on my hips and shoot him a withering glare. "You find that idea amusing?"

"I do, because you're this big." He holds up his hand level to his waist and bites back another laugh. "You're like a hyperactive chihuahua."

My only reply to his less-than-original insult is a roll of my eyes, which is apparently enough to bait the man.

"You need a sense of humor. I can't be the first guy to mention your size," he says with an offhanded shrug.

"You're not," I reply as I dig through the items stashed on the shelf. "Plenty of men have mentioned plenty of things where I'm concerned. Thanks for being just like them."

"Sweetheart, I'm nothing like any man you've ever known, and that kills you."

I ignore Asher's barb and focus on something more satisfying—something guaranteed to bring me a sliver of pleasure tonight. My hand closes around the bottle of whiskey, and I smile.

Knew you'd come in handy, beautiful.

Grabbing a spare glass, I carry the bottle to the worn couch and sit down, cross-legged.

Time to ignore the tatted heathen and focus on a cup of liquid heaven.

Asher strolls over to the couch, his hands shoved in his

pockets as he stares pointedly at the bottle. "Aren't you going to share?"

"No." To drive home my statement, I lift the glass to my lips and feel the sweet burn drift down my throat, my gaze never wavering from his face.

It seems that, despite trading taunts for the past fifteen minutes, my one-word retort is the final straw for Asher's temper. He throws his hands up, frustration twisting his mouth. "What is your fucking problem? Do you need to get laid or something?"

Bristling at his comment, I take another sip, letting a slow, satisfied hiss escape. "Now, *that's* some damn fine whiskey." I let the words hang, then shift my gaze to Asher, who appears practically apoplectic at my nonchalance. "And to answer your rude inquiry—one, it's none of your damn business. Two, even if I did, you'd be the *last* person I'd call. And three, you know what my fucking problem is."

"Yeah, some imaginary noise complaint on a night when the parlor was closed, along with accusing me of being a horrible person. Not sure how that happened when I hadn't even said hello to you. Guess you're the type to judge a book by its cover, huh?"

Jumping to my feet, I march over to him, jabbing my finger into his chest. "How dare you pretend nothing happened that night. I'm not imagining the things that man said to me—or the fact he claimed you told him what type of woman I was. Pretty surprising, considering I'd never even said hello to you."

Once again, I turn his words against him, but this time, he's not amused.

"Who are you talking about? Black Lotus was closed. I spoke with Braden and Zane about that night and neither of them was anywhere near here." Anger creases his face as his voice increases several decibels.

"It wasn't either of them."

Asher tugs a hand through his hair, yanking at the dark strands. "Then who? That's the extent of my staff."

I glide my hand along the back of my neck, allowing the memory of the man's ugly sneer to once again flood my brain. "I don't know his name. He was too busy insulting and threatening me to allow for a proper introduction. He wore some stupid band shirt and had a huge evil clown tattoo on his neck. It extended partway up his face. Totally grotesque."

In the next instant, the strangest thing happens. The anger in Asher's face slides away, replaced by a look of realization. "Micah." He glances away, releasing a frustrated breath through his nose. "I should have known."

"Should have known what?"

"Micah *wasn't* one of my employees, because I fired him earlier that same week. He claimed he lost the key to the shop, and I hadn't had a chance to change the locks."

I shrug, trying to deduce Asher's point. "He broke in?"

"Technically, yes. That's why he was such a dick to you. He figured you'd tell me, and I'd ream his ass out."

"Instead, you reamed my ass out."

He runs a hand over his jaw, a resigned grunt escaping his mouth. "To be fair, you gave as good as you got. What did the man say to you?"

"*Now* you want to know?"

He raises his hands in mock surrender. "I do, actually."

Although I doubt Asher will give two craps what nasty comments his former employee hurled my way, there's no harm in giving him the rundown—even if it is six months later.

I return to the couch and take a sip of whiskey, allowing the burn to cool my emotions. "It was late, so I went over to ask him to turn down the music, and he told me where I could shove my request. Then, he told me you had warned him how I was a prissy bitch and if I didn't march right back to my little store, you would both make me sorry."

Asher's eyes widen, a muscle jumping in his jaw. "What the fuck? Why didn't you tell me?"

I scoff, tempted to throw the bottle of whiskey at him. "I tried, remember? At which point, *you* called me several terms of endearment right in front of my patrons."

"You went off on me in front of my clients, too."

No way will I last the night without killing this man. "I had a reason."

"Well, I thought I did, too."

"You thought wrong." Then, much to my horror, a tear slides down my cheek. I swipe it away, hoping Asher didn't see it. That's all I need—the man thinking I'm a typical weak woman.

But Asher doesn't laugh or smirk. In a wholly unexpected move, he sits on the couch, pivoting to face me. "I didn't know he threatened you. Hell, I had no idea he was here that night."

There's something so soothing about Asher's voice now. Only moments earlier, it growled with authority and anger. Now, it's soft and reassuring, a tone one would use to address a scared animal.

Guess I'm the scared animal in this scenario.

"Now you know." I take another swallow of whiskey, widening my eyes when he raises a brow. "What?"

"Can I please have a glass? Like it or not, we're stuck down here tonight. Might as well make the best of it."

"I *am* making the best of it." Yes, I'm being petulant, but I refuse to share my whiskey without an apology.

Asher releases a noisy sigh, shooting me a side-eye. "Trust me, I'm not happy with Micah and when I see him again, I'll beat him to a pulp for what he said. No one threatens a woman, especially not one as tiny as you."

"Didn't you know? Hyperactive chihuahuas are pretty intimidating when provoked. We're like rats on speed."

Ash chuckles, a full grin spreading across his face. "My comment about your size rubbed you the wrong way, didn't it?"

I tuck my hair behind my ear and avert my gaze. "I've heard worse. Way worse."

He skews his mouth to one side. "If I'm being honest, I think your size is adorable."

Did the man just compliment me in some odd, offbeat fashion? Has the world tilted on its axis?

I stare at him, my mind struggling to process this surprising new side of Asher Hammond.

"If you keep looking at me like that, I might forget you're supposed to hate me." His tone is teasing, but there's a seriousness beneath it that my body can't ignore.

A flush climbs my cheeks, a wholly unexpected response to his intense gaze. "You're a fan of rats on speed? Unusual fetish. And despite my diminutive stature, I can take care of myself."

I'm not kidding. A woman living alone in the big city needs a few tricks up her sleeve. Hell, a woman living alone *anywhere* needs to know how to defend herself from undesirables.

"So, I've noticed, but I'm still kicking the shit out of Micah. He's an asshole."

"I thought that was my title. Or is it the Frost Queen? Wait, I'm the prissy bitch. Hard to keep up with your handbook of nicknames for me."

Asher presses his lips together, but I see the remorse coloring his features. First time I've witnessed that expression on his face. "I'm really not a bad guy. Ask anyone in town. I'm pretty well-liked across the board."

"Uh-huh. Is that an apology I'm hearing? No whiskey until you admit I'm not the harpy you thought I was." Swirling the alcohol in my glass, I study his face, searching for signs he's messing with me. But his green-gold gaze holds mine, with no hint of deceit.

"I'm sorry. I should have given you a chance to explain —fully—what happened that night, because no one should ever speak to you the way Micah did. Or the way I did, for that matter."

"I'll consider your request."

"One more thing. Ever heard the saying that things stop growing when they're perfect? You just got there sooner than most women." Asher waves his hand, gesturing along my form.

No, I'm not imagining it. He actually did compliment me.

Yes, the man has ulterior motives, but this is a side of Asher Hammond I have no idea how to handle.

"Damn, you really want a drink, don't you?" Despite the harshness of my words, I bite back a smile—a smile that Asher catches and returns.

"Desperate times."

With a fake glower, I grab the bottle and pour him a

glass. "Thank you for saving me earlier. I was really scared when that rung broke."

"I really wasn't going to let you fall." Asher accepts the glass of whiskey, but to my surprise, he sets it aside, extending his hand. "Can we start over? Properly this time? I'm Asher Hammond, but only you and my mother call me by my full name. And then, only when I'm in a crap ton of trouble. To everyone else, I'm Ash, the owner of Black Lotus and the micro farm on the edge of town. Contrary to previously held notions, I'm neither a heathen nor a hoodlum."

I stare at his outstretched hand, wondering if I should cave or cling to resentment. Truth be told, I'm a total softie and hate holding grudges—even when they're deserved.

After my father abandoned my mother and me, I spent far too many years clinging to anger and resentment. I learned the hard way there's no point in staying angry. You only hurt yourself that way.

With a sly grin, I shake his hand, his skin warm against mine. "Nice to meet you. Officially, this time."

"Now, it's your turn. That's how introductions work."

"You don't say." I grab a throw pillow and rest it on my lap. Hey, if Asher—I mean, Ash—turns back into a pumpkin, I can always make good on my broomstick threat. "I'm Oriana Thorne, owner of One More Page. Terrible with heights and broken ladders, but usually fearless beyond that. Quite a mouth on me, as you've already seen."

"Most definitely," Ash murmurs, his gaze dropping to my lips.

There's something tantalizing about the growly edge of his voice, the way it rolls over me, much like the feelings that rolled over me when he held me on the ladder.

I shift slightly, determined not to let Ash get under my skin. No, he does that with all the other women in town, and I will not be another tally mark in his black book.

"I also recently acquired a grand and slightly rundown manor house at auction. It was a spur-of-the-moment decision that's left me questioning my sanity. Oh, and everyone calls me Ori, unless they're you. Then it's Ms. Ice Queen."

"Your mouth never stops, does it?"

"Sometimes, when I'm otherwise occupied."

Shit, I realize how that sounds. Did I mean it like that? And did I mean for him to interpret it as a subtle innuendo?

Ash's brows raise and he nods his head slightly before reaching for his glass to take a swallow. "This is good whiskey."

Seems he isn't going to mention my quip, which is just as well.

"I have good taste."

"You do." He shifts in his seat, tossing his booted legs on the wobbly coffee table. "Tell me about this house you bought. Are you talking about the old Dean estate?"

"That's the one. It needs a ton of work, and I am not at all talented in that arena."

"Maybe you could scare it into submission with your temper." I shoot him a scowl, earning a chuckle in response. "I'm glad you bought the place. When it went up for auction, I was afraid some real estate developer would scoop it up, raze the house and split up the land."

"They might have had the right idea, honestly. The to-do list seems endless."

He leans forward, stroking his beard. "I can help you with the renovations."

"You're a carpenter, too?"

He dusts his fingers on his shirt, puffing out his chest. "I've got skills."

I sputter my whiskey at his brazen comment. "All sorts, I'm sure."

"I'm not denying it."

I roll my eyes, choking back a laugh. "Neither are most of the women in this town."

Hey, if he's taking the conversation down this path, I'll go along for the ride.

"What exactly *have* you heard about me? Actually, hold that thought."

Without waiting for my reply, Ash disappears to the far side of the basement, returning moments later with some pretzels and fruit. "I put a small fridge in earlier this year, and I always keep some food down here. Never thought I'd need it for an impromptu sleepover, but here we are."

"Look at you. Prepared for every situation."

"Like I said, I've got skills."

I'm sure you have many.

Leaning back against the couch, I let my gaze wander over Ash—*really* look at him for the first time since my arrival, and I understand Mina's fixation. The man is beautiful. He could be a model with his finely chiseled face and piercing eyes. Then, there's his body—no clothes in the world could hide the bulging muscles, all covered in colorful ink designs.

Totally not my type, but I see why women swoon over him.

"What really happened to your date? I can't imagine you end most evenings before eight o'clock."

Ash shrugs. "I called it off early. Had other things to do."

"Things or people?" I tease, the warmth of the whiskey loosening my tongue.

Ash sputters his drink, then returns my cheeky grin. "That smart mouth of yours is going to get you in trouble, sweetheart."

"Define trouble. I might just enjoy it."

Of course I'm pushing his buttons. Turns out, it's way more fun than I realized.

"I guarantee we would."

No, that wasn't a Freudian slip. Ash meant it exactly like that.

I have to hand it to him. The man is smooth when he turns on the charm.

Back to small talk, even if our other conversation is far more fun.

I take another sip of my drink. "I'm sorry your date was a disappointment. Do you have many of those?"

"Dates or disappointments?"

"I already know the answer to the first one. Everyone around here does."

"Now, you have to tell me what you've heard about me."

"Ash, you must know what the women say."

"I want to know what *you've* heard," he presses, shooting me a wink.

Tucking my legs under me, I take another sip of whiskey as the relaxation flows through me. Seems the weight of my long-standing gripe with Ash bothered me more than I realized. Now that it's in the past, I feel lighter.

"I'm not the only one with monikers. You have quite the handful of nicknames, too."

"Such as?"

I tap my finger against my chin, recalling all the rumors about Ash and his legendary prowess. Trust me, there have been a ton. "Lady killer, heartbreaker, king of the one-night stands. Shall I continue?"

I expect a knowing smirk, but Ash's eyes darken as his foot taps out an erratic rhythm against the floor. "Damn. I'm sorry I asked."

"Ash, people love you here in Sparkwood—ladies and men alike." I shrug, topping off his glass in a show of solidarity. "When it comes to you and me, it's safe to say we were both wrong about each other."

The smile returns to his face as he snaps his fingers. "Let's make it right. How about a game of truth or consequences? Great way to get to know each other."

"How about no?"

"Come on, Ori. We're here all night. What else are we going to do? Unless … you have a better idea?" Again, his gaze sweeps over me, his lower lip caught between his teeth.

I know that look. I've seen the man use it countless times on countless women.

It never fails to charm them right out of their pants.

I realize Ash is getting off on his flirtatious banter, no doubt certain he's getting to me. What he fails to understand is that, despite my bookworm appearance, I don't actually have a corkscrew wedged up my bum.

Just because I don't fall into bed with scads of men doesn't mean I'm incapable of having fun.

I *love* having a good time, especially when it involves messing with men whose egos and biceps are the size of tree trunks.

Surprise, surprise, Ash possesses both.

Time to turn Mr. Asher Hammond on his head, something I doubt many women have attempted.

Gliding my fingers along his biceps, I release a low purr. "I have tons of ideas, Ash. Question is, which one should I play with first?"

Shock passes across Ash's features at my come-hither approach, but he recovers quickly, that half-smirk decorating his mouth. "Tons, huh? Ori, this is an entirely new side of you."

"Ash, you don't know *any* side of me."

This time, his face remains impassive, but a flame sparks in his eyes. Seems I *am* getting to the man.

See? Way too much fun. Men who never have to work for a woman's attention don't know what to do when they're denied what they believe is a God-given right.

Asher Hammond is gorgeous, successful and, if the word on the street is to be believed, a king between the sheets.

But none of those characteristics will make me drop *my* knickers.

For me, sex is more than a physical act. It's a connection. If he doesn't stir something in me, he's not *getting* in me.

Still, this is a fun way to pass the evening, and he is some fine eye candy.

Ash leans against the sofa, resting his head in his hand. "Yet."

I scrunch my nose, shooting him a curious look. "What?"

"You claimed I don't know any side of you, Ori. I issued a qualifier. I may not know you *yet*, but that is about to change, love."

Chapter 6

The Space Between Us

Ash

A snort of laughter escapes Ori's mouth, but I catch a glimmer of mischief dancing in her eyes.

"What's so funny?"

She dismisses my inquiry with a wave of her hand, throwing in an eye roll for effect. "Have you *ever* had to work for a woman's affections?"

Her question hits the bull's-eye, even if I won't admit it aloud.

But I know one thing for certain—Oriana *won't* be one of those women.

That knowledge only makes her hotter, and trust me, even when I couldn't stand the sight of the woman, I sure as hell enjoyed watching her walk away.

Hey, a great ass is a great ass, and Ori's peach is magnificent.

Then again, so is the rest of her.

Ori pulls her legs from underneath her, pinning me with her dark gaze. "Are you ever going to ask?"

Her question throws me, especially considering where

my mind—and our conversation—has been treading. "About us having sex?"

She snorts again, a trait I find more adorable every time. "No, Ash. About my handy dandy signature, which I know you need. That's why you're here, isn't it? We both know it isn't for an impromptu sleepover."

There's something indelibly sexy about a woman who sees through the fluff and bullshit, aiming right for the heart of a situation. Ori has it in spades. "I consider the sleepover a bonus." At her incredulous look, I chuckle, realizing that *all* my usual tricks are getting me nowhere. "Have you heard any of the details about my plan for this space?"

"You want to open a bar, right?" Ori shrugs and captures her bottom lip between her teeth. Now I'm staring at her mouth again.

What the hell were we talking about? Braden is right—this woman has me all kinds of mixed up.

What is it about her?

Clearing my throat, I force myself to remain on topic. Good luck convincing my dick of that idea. "Not just a bar. A modern-day speakeasy. A private club, open once or twice per week, complete with live music, dancing, and beverages from the Roaring '20s."

Ori drags her tongue along her lower lip, marinating on the idea. Granted, her sexy as fuck gesture has me marinating on something else entirely.

Definitely not helping my dick situation.

At all.

"What do you think?"

"This is your concept?"

"My adaptation, anyway." Narrowing my eyes, I try to interpret her silence. "Why do you look so surprised?"

"You hit me as more of a biker bar aficionado. No offense."

Her remark irks the hell out of me. I get why she believes that way, even though it's total nonsense. Stiffening, I kick my booted legs onto the worn coffee table with a frustrated huff. "That's all you see, isn't it? I'm covered in ink and ride a hog, so I must be part of an MC, right? Some fringe members of society who may or may not be involved in illegal activities? For your information, F. Scott Fitzgerald is my favorite author, and I want to bring back some small piece of the glory that was his heyday." Another grunt flies from my mouth as I grab my glass of whiskey. "Probably a stupid idea, anyway."

What most people don't see behind my tough-guy facade is the sensitive man existing on the periphery. A man who, despite all the bed bunnies and accolades in the tattoo industry, has never quite felt good enough—a man who hides that insecurity behind a devil-may-care attitude.

Most times, it works like a charm. But for some reason, I find myself wanting Ori's approval, and not just because I require her legal release.

I want a woman like Oriana to see that potential in me. To look past the tattoos and hardened exterior and glimpse the man inside … the one I let no one else see.

"It's *not* a stupid idea, Ash. In fact, I was looking around the space just before you arrived and thinking how the walls still whisper their secrets. She deserves a renaissance, and I think you're the man for the job."

"Now you're patronizing me."

Ori scoots closer and grabs my hand, her slight fingers entwined around mine. "It was a thoughtless comment that I never should have said. Trust me, I know there is so much more to you than tattoos and motorcycles. The speakeasy idea is brilliant, and the only issue I see is ensuring my late nights don't interfere with yours, and vice versa."

I hear her speaking, fully aware she's given me the green light, but I'm preoccupied by the feel of her hand in mine. Her skin is like silk, compared to my calloused palms, and I wonder if the rest of her body is this soft.

"Ash?"

Snapping from my daze, I relax into a smile, even daring to lift her palm against my mouth to press a kiss to her skin. "We misjudged each other, all because of a seedy asshole named Micah. One who will sport several bruises after I see him again."

"He's not worth it."

"He is, because I missed out on six months of knowing you."

"On the flip side, you had six months to plot my demise," Ori replies with a grin. "Don't deny it. We've both thought up a hundred ways to make the other disappear."

I clear my throat and shrug as I bite back a laugh. "None of which will be carried out, right? I know how tough you are, Little One, and I'm not sure I'm brave enough to continue messing with you."

Truth? I love messing with her. She keeps me entertained because I'm never sure *what* will come out of her luscious mouth next.

Although now I'm thinking of tons of ways to keep her wicked tongue occupied.

Fuck. Get it together, man.

Trouble is, I'm not sure I can. My insides are a tightly coiled spring, quivering with nervous energy.

Maybe it's because we're no longer sworn enemies.

Or maybe because she's on board with the speakeasy idea.

My life can return to its aforementioned routine now, but that life suddenly doesn't hold the same appeal.

The thrill I'm getting from holding her hand—wait a damn minute. I'm *still* holding her hand.

It's just like those lost moments on the ladder, when everything but her faded from view.

As if reading my thoughts, Ori glances down at our entwined fingers before slipping her hand from my grasp.

She straightens her spine, allowing a few inches of space between us. "Well, that's settled. All in all, a successful evening. We no longer detest one another, and I'll sign whatever documentation Kiki requires."

But I'm nowhere near finished. Now that I've spent some time with this petite beauty, I know one thing.

I need more.

Much, much more.

"We got business out of the way and now, the fun can start." I clink her glass, my eyes tracing the lines of her body. Ori may not be my usual type, but she's one of the most gorgeous women I've ever seen.

And if I'm not mistaken, the feeling is mutual.

Ori quirks a brow, her dark eyes dancing behind her glasses. "Dare I ask what you have in mind?"

Oh, beautiful, I wish you would.

I fully realize I need to take my libido down a few notches before I overtake her slight frame and show her just how much fun we can have together.

Leaning forward, I rest my arms on my knees, my famous smirk playing about my mouth. Am I pulling out all the stops? Damn right I am. "I already told you. We get to know one another. Time for truth or consequences."

She sputters her drink at my request. "Ash, I haven't played that game since high school."

"See? Entirely too long. Come on, we're here all night. Let's make the most of it."

What I don't mention is how I'd far rather strip off her clothes and explore *her* all night … but I will. First, I have to break through her cool and collected exterior, because I sense the fire underneath. I felt it when I held her against me in the bookstore.

All she needs is someone willing to stoke it to life.

Plus, Ori wears some pretty thick emotional armor. Hell, it's almost as thick as mine, but I want to dig deep and get to know the woman *beneath* that protective shell.

Part of me wonders if anyone ever has.

With a shrug, Ori flops back against the couch, a smile easing across her face. "Fine. You go first."

THE BEST PART ABOUT THESE SILLY GAMES IS HOW QUICKLY the time flies when you're engaged in good-natured ribbing and laughter. We spend the next hour learning the basics about one another—schooling, childhood, marital status, kids—all the while blowing each other's minds with how wrong we had the other pegged.

First impressions are often that way, particularly when based on outward appearances.

Still, I know there are way more layers to Oriana Thorne. Time to jump to the good stuff.

Stroking my chin, I shoot her a mischievous grin. "Where's one place you had sex that everyone said you should try, but you hated?"

A low giggle rises from Ori's chest, her tongue once again gliding along her lower lip. By far, the most unintentionally sexy move I've ever seen.

Don't get me wrong. Plenty of women employ that maneuver, but Ori has it mastered. Best part? She has no clue how unhinged she's making me.

I'm certain Oriana Thorne is the quintessential good girl. Sure, she might enjoy a spanking or the occasional porn flick, but all in all, she's pretty vanilla.

There's nothing wrong with vanilla—except when women insist they're anything but, and you end up learning the hard way that they are.

Trust me, I've been with enough women to know that's a fact. And it works both ways—men who crow about the size of their cock rarely have anything to brag about.

That's why I don't brag. My hookups do it for me.

I keep quiet. More of a show than tell kind of guy.

"I see we've segued to sex talk," Ori says, sputtering her whiskey as she takes a sip.

"It's always interesting."

With a grin, she gestures to herself. "Not when you think I'm an old maid who fucks through a sheet."

See? Totally vanilla. At least she admits the fact.

Chuckling, I shake my head. "Answer the question."

"Easy. Airplane bathroom."

Or ... not vanilla at all.

"You did not fuck in an airplane bathroom," I scoff, dismissing her claim with a wave of my hand.

But Ori's shrug and unaffected gaze tell me she most definitely *did* join the mile high club. Hell, even I haven't checked that one off my bucket list.

"I did. Really tight space even for my tiny body. Do not recommend."

"Was this with your boyfriend at the time?"

"Not exactly. The co-pilot." Ori giggles at my shocked expression. "Just because *you* think I'm a prissy bitch doesn't mean you're right."

"Few women surprise me."

"Are you saying I'm not typical?"

"In any way. Huh." Yes, I'm floored by her admission. I'm also pretty fucking turned on. Sitting up, I shift on the couch, trying to adjust myself without Oriana catching on.

Judging by the mischievous smirk on her face, she knows exactly what I'm doing. "You okay over there?"

"I don't know. You care to help me out?"

"You've never been told no, have you?"

"Not true. I got rejected a ton as a teenager, but then I started paying attention to women. Picking up on the subtle cues—the intangible signs that they're interested. After a while, I got damn good at it."

"And what cues are you picking up from me?" Ori inquires, resting her head on her hand, expectant curiosity on her face.

"That you have no intention of falling for any of my lines, even if you are attracted to me."

"Is that a fact?"

I shift again, those dark eyes of hers boring holes into

my visage. Talk about an intense gaze. "Honestly, it's a guess. You're hard to read, Ori."

Now the corners of that gorgeous mouth curl up. "Thought you were good at reading women."

Tossing up my hands, I shoot her an embarrassed grin. "Not you, apparently. But you're nothing like the women I'm used to."

Ori stiffens, her eyes cutting to an innocuous spot on the floor. "Got it."

Shit, it was a compliment—one that went over like a lead balloon. "That's a good thing, Ori."

She releases a sigh before meeting my gaze. "It's just I've heard that exact line so many times regarding me. How I'm a tough nut to crack and not worth the effort. And I know they're not all wrong."

"Actually, that's exactly what they are. The wrong guys."

"Well, I've had my share of the wrong guys, so I'm thinking the right one isn't out there. Maybe I should take a page from your playbook and sample all the wares in Sparkwood."

"Absolutely not."

"Why not? Seems like you have a good time."

Do I, though? If you asked me earlier today, the answer would have been a resounding yes.

Lots of fun times. Lots of women.

Lots of moments that didn't equal up to anything special.

Unlike right now, where I'm hanging on Ori's every word, truly blown away by every facet of this woman.

And I have yet to discover my favorite facets—on her.

"Casual sex isn't your style. You've got toys for that." I

lean in, feeling the tension crackling in the air like a live wire. "You want it all. No exceptions."

Her eyes widen at my words. I've hit the nail on the damn head.

"Easier said than done."

"Easy as fuck with the right man. The right guy won't think you're too much. He'll think you're perfect."

Ori rolls her eyes, but I catch the hint of a smile playing on her mouth. She appreciates my sentiment, even if she won't admit it aloud.

"Your turn, Ori. Hit me with a good one."

She cocks her head, skewing her mouth to the right. "Let's see. Okay, I've got one. What's your weakness, and don't say you don't have one. *Everyone* has one, even big tatted bad boys like you."

Lifting my glass, I nod in her direction. "Right now, my weakness is a tiny librarian type who, I suspect, knows exactly how sexy she is—but would sooner die than admit it."

Her eyes widen, a spark of fire igniting in their depths before she masks it with a practiced smirk and a snap of her fingers. "You're damn good at delivering those lines, Asher Hammond. Right on cue. Smooth as hell."

Shaking my head, I release a frustrated grunt. For once, my words weren't meant to butter a woman up. They were the truth. "A woman who also apparently still hates me, contrary to what she's said otherwise."

"I don't hate you. I barely know you, although we are working on that. Now, answer the damn question."

"I just did."

A slight flush colors her cheeks, upping the ante on her

cuteness factor. "Fine, but since I don't believe you, I get to go again. What's your biggest hang-up?"

Downing some whiskey, I shrug. "I suppose it would be the fact that I don't date."

"You mean, you don't call it dating? I've seen you with scads of women around town."

Nodding, I focus on my glass, feeling like a fraud for the first time in years. "It's never serious. I'm a lone wolf."

Why do I care what this woman thinks of me? What is going on in my damn brain?

"Wolves travel in packs," Ori adds, her expression smug.

"True, but I've got my boys for that."

"They also mate for life."

Scoffing, I fix her with my green-gold gaze, shaking my head in disbelief. "You have an answer for everything."

"Just calling you on your bullshit."

Her observation makes my back go up. I can't be sure if she's hit a sore spot, or I'm pissed she reads me this well in such a short amount of time. "Okay, Ms. Smarty Pants, why do *you* think I don't date?"

"You're scared."

Chapter 7

Unwritten Fire

Ash

"**N**ot even close." I bite out a laugh, downing the last of my whiskey.

Time for a refill, or I could forgo the glass and chug the damn liquid from the bottle.

"I'm serious. You're terrified that a woman could wrap herself around your heart and set up residence."

Drumming out an erratic rhythm on the table, I clear my throat, feeling my ire rise. "Sorry to disappoint you, but that's not the case. Love and romance are two words I don't use. Not now, not ever."

I'm not sure what emotion I expect, but the sympathetic expression crossing Ori's face isn't one of them. "I could argue your statement and tell you that one day you might believe differently, but that would be a moot point, wouldn't it? Instead, I'll simply nod in agreement and swiftly change the subject."

"Why are you changing the subject?"

Her eyes widen. "It's obviously a touchy one for you. Someone has hurt you at some point. No one starts out the gate detesting the idea of love. I'm sorry someone treated you poorly."

"Doesn't matter." I mutter the words, hating how easily Ori sees through my facade.

Or maybe she's the first woman to bother looking for the cracks.

Either way, she's right. Once upon a time, I believed in love—fully and madly bought into the whole concept. Even got down on one knee and asked the woman to marry me. That's when she informed me that marriage wasn't an option—namely, because she was already married.

Nice of her to tell me six months into the relationship.

C'est la vie.

After that fiasco, I shelved the idea of true love and soulmates.

Since then, my bed has remained warm and my heart intact.

I plan to keep it that way.

"Can I go again?"

Ori's voice jerks me from my reverie, and I nod, pouring some more whiskey in preparation. "You're hijacking this game, beautiful, but go ahead. Another deep and philosophical inquiry?"

"Not at all. An easy one. How many piercings do you have?"

Thank God, it *is* an easy question.

"Six ... no wait, seven."

"I see three." Ori motions to my head, referring to my earrings and nose ring.

"My nipples and—" I stick out my tongue, running the bar along my teeth.

Now it's Ori's turn for the slight bodyweight shift. Seems I'm unhinging her, too. "Ah, interesting."

"I haven't heard any complaints. Great for all manner of dining."

A cocky aside? Yes, but I need a segue from the heavy talk.

Ori giggles, a slight flush coloring her face. "Is that a fact?"

"It is."

"That's still only six piercings."

I pause for effect, knowing this one will shock the hell out of a woman like Oriana. Hopefully, in *all* the right ways. "My cock."

Those huge brown eyes widen, her jaw slackening at my answer. "You're joking."

"Nope. Want to see?" I slide my fingers beneath my waistband, tugging it down just enough to tease, giving her a hint but letting her imagination fill in the rest.

Will I show her if she responds in the affirmative? Damn straight, I will.

I'm going to push the envelope.

Starting now.

"Is that your standard line?" she asks.

"I don't need lines."

She captures her lower lip between her teeth, making my dick strain against my jeans.

"Doesn't that make sex a painful undertaking?"

I lean forward, inching ever closer to her. "No, sweetheart. It makes it fabulous."

"For you or me?"

Now, we're getting somewhere.

"For us both. Admit it, you're curious."

Ori fumbles with the clasp holding her hair, her long locks tumbling over her shoulders.

Fuck, but she's beautiful.

"I'm intrigued. Women like me, you know, us staid prissy types, don't play with many hot, pierced men."

I quirk a brow at her, my come-hither smile adorning my face. *Thanks for the ego boost, doll.* "You think I'm hot?"

"I think you know you are."

"Here's the thing. I don't give a shit what anyone else thinks or believes, okay? I want to know what *you* think."

She huffs out a breath, her cheeks reddening under my intense scrutiny.

No way you're getting away from this conversation, Ori. You started it.

"Well?"

"You're goddamn gorgeous, okay? Even though, until recently, I held some not very nice thoughts about you."

"How about now?"

The flush on her cheeks intensifies, and she looks away. "Can we talk about something else?"

Knew it.

I knew she felt it, too.

"Sure, as soon as you answer the question."

"I've had thoughts, even though I'm aware I'm not *your* type. There. You happy now?"

Her response irks the hell out of me. With a growl, I move closer, brushing my leg against hers. "See? That's proof you don't know me."

"You told me not an hour ago that I wasn't your type."

I shrug, leaning in to catch a hint of her delicious scent again. "You're not, but that doesn't mean I don't think you're sexy as fuck, Ori."

I half expect her to inch away, but it seems her body is as desperate as mine.

That fire I hoped to stoke? Baby, it's burning.

"You're telling me the big, tatted motorcycle man likes the mousy librarian type?" I see the doubt in her eyes, as her gaze roams over my face, searching for a sign that I'm messing with her.

All she has to do is look at the pronounced bulge in my pants to know I'm deadly serious.

"No. I'm telling you that I like *you*. I'm going to kiss you and not stop until we're both naked and I'm buried inside you."

A pant flies from her lips, and it's one of the sexiest sounds I've heard all night.

"Any objections?"

I swear to God, if she gives me the go-ahead, she will be naked within thirty seconds. I'm that desperate for her at this point.

Ori chews on the inside of her lip before shaking her head. "I'm not looking to be another name on your list, Ash."

Truth is, I'm not looking for her to be one. I'm not sure what's happening between us, but I know I don't want to stop. "There is no fucking list. There's you and me. Right here. Right now. I promise, I'll love you like no one ever has before. What do you think?"

"Whose turn is it?"

My face splits into a grin at her attempted diversion.

Not a chance, beautiful. We're seeing this one through to fruition.

I grab the pillow Ori is using to shield herself, tossing it on the floor as I move up the length of her body. Balancing my weight on my forearms, I nuzzle her lips with the slightest caress. "It's my turn. Tell me what you want, Oriana. Tell me what you want me to do to you."

Her entire body trembles, but I feel the heat rising from her skin.

Once again, her intoxicating scent fills my nostrils, beckoning me closer.

Never close enough.

Dipping my head, I press a kiss at the base of her ear, my breath delivering a delicious tickle. "What do you want?"

"Everything." Her words are barely a whisper, but they're all I need to hear.

My original plan? To drizzle a few kisses along her ivory skin and leave her begging for more. But the moment my tongue glides along her neck, tasting her warmth, I'm done for.

The tables turn and all I feel is her body as she strains toward me. By the time I capture her kiss, Ori owns me.

My new mission for the evening? Spending every second until daylight, loving every inch of her. Making her mine.

Ori's arms twine about my neck as she pulls herself closer, her tits mashing against my chest.

My mouth claims hers, my hand slipping into her hair as my tongue teases her with all the ways I plan to please her tonight.

But just like with everything else, the woman gives as good as she gets. Ori returns the kiss with a fierceness that is pure fire, as her fingers glide along my sinewy muscle.

Gliding my fingers under her shirt, I play along the soft skin of her abdomen before skimming the material over her head. I can't keep the smile from my mouth as I drink in her full breasts, barely contained by her purple lace bra.

She reaches for the button on her pants, but I stay her hand.

"Let me do it. I want full control."

"You realize I want a turn, too, right?"

"Fuck yes, Ori, you will get a turn. There's no way I'm missing a chance to have that gorgeous mouth wrapped around my cock."

"Gorgeous and talented," she purrs, dragging her lips along my neck and setting off an array of sparks. "But I'll let you be the judge."

What is it about this woman? Her every word drives me closer to the edge, and I haven't even tasted her yet.

I pull off her pants, my cock hardening to the point of pain. The woman can't weigh over 110 pounds, but she's got full breasts, a juicy ass and hips just made for holding. How the hell does such a tiny woman rock such incredible curves?

All I know is I'm damn thankful she does.

My gaze wanders over the matching lingerie. Yet another unexpected pleasure Oriana is gifting me.

"Damn, but you are full of surprises."

"What did you expect? Cotton briefs?"

"Honestly, it wouldn't have mattered, but this is fucking hot, Ori. You are a spectacularly gorgeous woman."

A flush crawls up her body, only upping her sexiness. Seems despite her supposedly storied past, I still get to her.

Good, because she is sure as hell getting to me. In all the best ways.

"You like?"

"Very much, although I prefer them on the floor.

Nothing is coming between me and this amazing body." I grab her ankles, gliding my hands along her soft skin as I drag that expensive lingerie down her legs and toss it over my shoulder to fully drink her in.

Laid out, and mine for the taking.

Shapely legs lead up to a perfect pussy, ripe for the tasting. Leaning in, I drag my tongue along Ori's slick skin, as a low moan falls from her mouth.

My hands slide under that delectable ass as I bury my face between her thighs, breathing in her sweet siren scent. Fuck, but Oriana is all woman, and by the end of the night, there won't be an inch of her I haven't explored. Circling my tongue around her clit, I smile at her heated groan as her hands knit in my hair.

"You want more?"

"If you stop now, I'll kill you on principle."

A dry chuckle escapes my mouth. "Works for me. I'll give you everything."

I mean it, too.

My goal is always to leave a woman satisfied, but with Ori, it's different. I want to love her so well that she never recovers.

She'll always remain as desperate as she is at this moment.

As we both are.

Ori doesn't hold back, her thighs clenching around my head as I show her *all* the bonuses of a tongue ring. Fuck, but she tastes good, like honey in my mouth.

A hum of satisfaction slips from her lips as I busy myself tasting her sweetness.

Just wait until I slide inside her.

She'll be begging for everything I've got to give.

"Ash, please make me come," Ori urges, her dark eyes daring me to deliver on my promise.

But despite her pleas, I won't rush. It's too much fun drawing this out, working her body into a frenzy of feelings.

I eat every inch of her delicious pussy, sinking my fingers into her wetness to stroke her deep and slow while my tongue teases her clit. I'll lick her all night until she passes out from the overwhelming ache, knowing that at this moment, I own her every thought.

Tortured moans squeeze past her mouth, and shivers rip through her body as I spend the next several minutes driving her wild.

"Ash, please. I'm begging you."

What a lady wants, a lady gets.

Ori's body bows under the force of her orgasm, her nails dragging across my skin with such ferocity there will be marks for days.

If it were any other woman, I'd be pissed about the scratches. But with Ori, I crave them. I want her marks on me, just as I want to mark her body for my own.

I move up her body, savoring the sight of her beneath me.

Fuck, but she's a vision—flushed skin, hair spread out against the pillow, a sated breath escaping her lips.

Ori runs a hand through her hair, a husky chuckle rising from her chest. "Now, I get what all the fuss is about."

"You like?" Grazing my lips along the column of her throat, I latch on, sucking that silky ivory skin as she writhes beneath me.

"Ash, Ash."

Every time she says my name, it revs me up a bit more.

Pulling back, I note the purplish area prominently displayed on her neck.

Childish? Maybe, but I'm sure as hell not sorry I did it.

"You marked me, didn't you?" Her dark eyes drill into me, a sassy grin crossing her face.

See? I knew she'd take it well.

I belt out a laugh as I feel for the claw marks on my shoulders and upper back. "Returning the favor, beautiful. These scratches will take a while to heal."

"I could apologize, but I'm not sorry." Ori repositions herself, wrapping her shapely stems around my waist. "In fact, I'm just getting started. And now, it's my turn."

I've found my new best friend. No question.

With a quick nip to her neck, I jump to my feet and yank off my boots and jeans.

But Ori isn't content to lie back and watch. With a catlike grace, she moves to my side, kneeling before me, those brown eyes wide with anticipation.

Funny, I've never had sex with a woman wearing glasses before. Let me tell you, with Ori, it's the hottest thing in the world.

My personal sexy librarian.

Looping her fingers in the waistband of my boxers, she pulls them down, my erect cock now only inches from her gorgeous mouth. "Well, you are just exquisite, aren't you?"

When she dances her tongue along my tip, I damn near lose it. I've been riding on that edge since I first touched her, and I'm not sure how much more I can handle.

But Ori senses my need, and in true fashion, sets out to push me past the brink of sanity. Wrapping her hands around my hips, she takes me into her mouth.

All of me.

Without a doubt, the most amazing mouth on the planet.

I wind my hand in her hair, meeting her sexually heated gaze. "You like my cock, don't you?"

Ori hums out her response, her fingers tightening against my skin while her tongue continues to work me over.

No way can I hold out much longer, and I need to be inside her. Need to feel that warmth surround me and threaten to drown me whole.

With a grunt, I step back from her oh-so-talented mouth, pulling her up from her knees. I guide her to the couch, easing her down into the cushions before reaching for a condom from my wallet. Rolling it down my length, I spread her legs wide, positioning myself to claim her.

"I was hoping you had one of those," Ori murmurs, scratching her fingers against my scalp as I slide my shaft through her wetness.

"Somehow, I doubt it would have stopped us."

I always practice safe sex. *Always.* But with Oriana, throwing caution to the wind is a very tempting proposition.

With a huffed breath, I fill her, moans escaping us both as I bury myself to the hilt.

How does she feel so damn good?

So damn right?

Squelching these thoughts, I focus instead on her beauty, her hips meeting my every thrust, her face awash with the same passion I know lines my face.

"You are so tight," I mutter, gritting my teeth against the building sensation.

She squeezes her sweet pussy around me, damn near

causing me to lose my last vestiges of control. "We're a perfect fit."

"Fuck yes, we are."

Ori continues milking my cock as I plow into her, both of us intent on driving the other mad with lust.

With a strangled cry, I explode, my vision going black. Beneath me, Oriana rides out her own orgasm, her cries echoing off the concrete walls.

I roll to one side, desperate to catch my breath after the greatest lay of my life.

Glancing into her face, I run a hand over my beard. "I think you've ruined me."

She raises up on one elbow, pressing kisses to my chest. "Will you forgive me if I promise to do it again and again?"

I chuckle before claiming her delightfully dirty mouth.

What a night this turned out to be.

Here I thought Oriana was my nemesis.

Turns out she's a dream come true. A very, *very* wet dream.

The truth hits like a sledgehammer, but I will the thought away before it can set up permanent camp in my brain.

I never hated Oriana. I hated she didn't feel for me what I felt for her the moment I saw her.

Now, I have a million feelings. Feelings I haven't allowed myself in over a decade.

Feelings I *can't* allow myself, no matter how perfect a fit Oriana and I are.

Time to rein in these overwhelming emotions.

Christ, I have women throw themselves at me on the daily and have zero issue holding them—or my libido— at bay.

But this woman is a different story.

The few times I've dared to look into her eyes, I got lost in their depths.

I don't lose myself to any woman.

Not after the last time.

No matter how exquisite a woman Ori may be, this ends in the morning.

There is no other option.

Chapter 8

The Morning After

Ori

I stretch, a low groan escaping my mouth at the effort. Blinking my eyes open, I scan the room, a momentary rush of panic shooting through me.

Where the hell am I?

Then I remember—the basement beneath my bookstore.

Where I spent the night with Asher Hammond.

Not just *any* night, either. That man certainly lives up to his reputation, and then some.

Damn, what a talented tongue. What a talented … everything.

Glancing to my left, I see the man of the hour is still asleep, his breathing soft and even. After our second round, we created a makeshift bed on the floor, complete with couch cushions and a blanket I swiped from my decorations box.

Let's just say it saw its share of action last night.

I skew my mouth to the side, taking a moment to drink in the man who rocked my world the night before.

"You, sir, are trouble with a capital T," I whisper, dragging my finger down his nose and holding back the giggle when Ash grumbles under his breath.

I slide from under his arm and pad to the bathroom to assess the damage. Thankfully, my headache is tolerable, even without coffee.

Guess amazing sex cuts down on hangovers.

Flipping on the light, I glimpse my reflection and realize amazing sex does wonders for *all* parts of me.

Instead of looking haggard, my face is rosy, my eyes bright. Okay, my hair is a bit of a disaster, but a few pulls through my long locks help to tame the massive length.

Not too bad.

When I roll my neck to work out the kinks that set up residence, I spy Ash's handiwork in the mirror. Large and purple, the hickey stands out in bass relief against my pale skin.

"Monster," I mutter with a grin.

Thank God it's winter and no one will question me wearing a turtleneck.

Spying a bottle of mouthwash, I take advantage. It's not a toothbrush, but at least my breath won't wake the dead.

When I exit the bathroom, Ash is awake, his head propped on his hand, a smile playing across his handsome face.

"Damn, but you're even more beautiful in the morning."

As the flush climbs my cheeks, I wave my hand in his direction, dismissing his compliment.

Ash, for his part, is undeterred. "Don't do that. You know you look good."

I kneel on our makeshift bed and reach over Ash to

grab my bra. "I know an epic romp certainly increases the blood flow."

With lightning-quick reflexes, Ash grabs my waist, rolls on top of me, and tangles his tongue with mine in a greedy, possessive kiss. "Epic, huh? I like that description." He moves his mouth along the column of my throat, while his fingers drift between my thighs to find their mark. "I see someone is ready for another round."

Two can play that game. I drag my gaze down the length of Ash's body, resting on his fully erect cock. "Seems I'm not the only one."

"Are you kidding? I've been ready." Ash reaches for his wallet, pulling out a foil package.

I'm beyond grateful Ash carries ample protection because we've made use of them, although another part of my psyche shudders to know how often he has to restock his supply.

Brain, you are not welcome in this moment. You can chastise me later. Right now, I'm all about the pleasure.

"How many of those do you carry at one time?"

Ash smirks as he rolls the condom down his impressive length. "This is it, so any additional epic romps are going to be raw, darling."

I hate how incredible that sounds.

Incredibly dangerous. Reckless. Delicious.

What is it about this man that makes me want to throw caution to the wind?

Ash settles between my thighs, his cock gliding against my skin and once again awakening every cell in my body.

"Do not make me wait, Asher Hammond."

A cocky grin stretches his face before he buries himself

inside me. Then he claims my mouth, swallowing every whimper as my legs tighten around him.

So good. So amazingly good.

The man was right. Cock rings are an amazing invention.

Then again, his cock would be remarkable with or without a piercing.

"Fuck, but I love your pussy, Ori." Ash growls out the words against my neck, his breath hot against my skin.

"She's kind of fond of you, too."

"Good thing, because my appetite for you is insatiable."

The man is relentless, pulling back to tease my entrance before filling me again, his hands wrapped around my hips for added leverage.

I fist the sheets, meeting his every thrust, my body being pushed ever closer to the edge. I'm right there.

Right there—

"Hey Ash, are you down here?"

We freeze mid-stroke at the unexpected—and *highly* unwelcome—male voice echoing down the steps.

Seems our fun little interlude is over.

Ash huffs out a breath before shooting me a look of resignation. "I'm down here, Braden. We got locked in last night. Have to fix that door."

Heavy footfalls sound on the wooden stairs as Ash scrambles to pull the blanket over our naked forms.

"Braden, give me a minute, okay?"

Too late.

"Why? What are you doing?"

Glancing up, I watch the bemused expression crossing Braden's face when he spies us together.

Talk about being caught with our pants down. Or in

this case, scattered all over the floor. Hey, we had priorities, and laundry wasn't one of them.

"Never mind. I see you two … are busy. Good morning, Oriana."

"Morning, Braden." Holy hell, my face is on fire. "We'll be right up."

"Take your time." Braden's smirk widens, earning glares from Ash and me. "I'll let Mina know you're okay. She came into Black Lotus this morning, panicking because the window display wasn't finished. When she realized your truck was still in the lot, she went into full on meltdown mode."

Crap, the window display. Looks like I'm pulling a double today. "Let her know where I am."

"No problem."

Braden is halfway up the stairs when Ash calls out to his brother. "Braden, no need to tell Mina or anyone else *all* the details, okay? Use some discretion, please."

I don't know why, but Ash's demand for secrecy sits as comfortably as my ass on a bed of porcupine quills. Pushing myself to sitting, I snatch my shirt, pulling it over my head.

Ash, meanwhile, rolls onto his back, scrubbing his face with his hands. "So much for a morning fix. Unless you want to make your customers wait a few extra minutes."

Oh no, you don't get an encore now, Mr. Hammond.

"You wanted to keep this situation discreet, Ash, and I'm hardly a quiet lover." I wrap my hair into a makeshift bun, certain I look like I've survived a hurricane, but desperate to get upstairs and away from … whatever this was.

One-night stand, Ori. That's the term you're looking for.

Why does that knowledge even bother me? Must be the

leftover glow from several orgasms. Ash is a fantastic lover, just like all his women claim, so of course I'm going to want more than one helping.

But, if Ash's reputation with women is to be believed, the man doesn't have a taste for leftovers.

I am now a leftover.

Yuck.

"Hey, get back here. You don't have to fly upstairs. They know we're okay, so there's no need to run away from me." Ash grips my upper arm, but I shirk his grasp and tug on my pants in a frenzied bid to escape.

"I have a business to run, as do you—a business with customers who don't appreciate waiting, especially when the delay is because of the owners being caught sans clothing."

He stands in all his naked glory, and I do my best *not* to ogle his muscled physique. I fail in said quest. Sue me. He's beautiful, and he knows it.

Ash closes the small distance between us, hoisting my now dressed form into his arms. "I didn't mean to offend you, Ori. You're not some secret I want to hide away, but I believe my private life should be just that—private. Who I spend my time with, and how we pass that time, isn't anyone's business but ours."

Damn, but he's good. Seems Asher has damage control on lockdown.

The worst part? I don't want him to know how disap-pointed I am that our time is over. I don't want to be *that* woman—fawning all over this tattooed god.

He has enough of those women, and I have my pride.

Forcing a smile, I steal a kiss, pulling back before Ash has a chance to lock me into another embrace. "I agree.

The last thing either of us needs is anyone giving us crap about last night."

"You're not mad?" His look is questioning, trying to gauge if my reaction is real or a thin veneer to protect hurt feelings.

"Not at all. Just craving caffeine."

"I hear you make a mean cup. I'll have to drop in at some point and try it."

"On the house."

Ash sets me down, nodding toward the stairs. "Go ahead. I'll be up soon."

Ah, can't walk up together, either. That would be too obvious. Yet another fact that sticks in my craw.

I pause at the bottom of the stairs, knowing this is my last chance before our moment is past.

How do I do this? I've never, not once, engaged in a one-night stand. Hey, I love having a good time, but I reserve my affections for people who want me for more than one round.

But what if Ash is as nervous as I am? What if he's waiting for me to make the first move?

What the hell. I've always been a woman who goes for what she wants. Why stop now?

With a steadying breath, I prepare to make a total ass of myself, whilst sending up a silent prayer that I don't. "I had a wonderful time. Actually, I don't remember ever having this much fun before."

"Me, too." Ash's gaze focuses on me like a laser, but I must push through.

"We should get locked in together again sometime. Or try something different, like dinner."

Ash nods but averts his gaze as he pulls a hand through his hair. "Always a possibility."

And there it is, the official blow-off.

I have joined the ranks of countless other women and, just like them, failed to be anything more than a footnote in Asher Hammond's black book.

Talk about mortification at its finest.

"Right. Well, bye." A full body flush breaks out across my body at his response, but I manage a last smile before dashing up the stairs.

Once inside One More Page, I make a beeline for the bathroom. Staring in the mirror, I blink away the tears welling in my eyes.

Don't you dare, Oriana. You knew what kind of man Asher Hammond was. Hell, he told you he doesn't believe in love or relationships. You just didn't listen.

"You will *not* be one of those women, moping about after a man," I hiss at my reflection. "You're going to go home, clean up, and then hurry back here to get your ass in gear. You have a store to run and a life to live. Asher Hammond was a one-time deal. The deal is done."

Time to get my head on straight and back to the business at hand.

Namely, pretending last night never happened.

How hard can it be? Sure, it was great sex, but it's not like I'll *never* have incredible sex again.

Maybe it was only memorable since I haven't had a decent lay since arriving in Sparkwood six months ago. Yes, that's got to be the reason.

And now, I can pursue an equally brilliant fuck with a far more attainable conquest. Asher Hammond is *not* the last of his kind.

Easy come, easy go.

What a complete and utter load of horseshit.

With a deep, centering breath, I yank open the bathroom door.

"Morning, Mina. Sorry I worried you," I call out toward the main part of the store before dashing to my office.

"I suppose I'll forgive you. On one condition." Her voice echoes down the hall, but I note the lilt in her tone.

No way, my darling friend. I'm not having *that* conversation right now. The sting of Ash's blow-off is far too fresh to discuss.

I grab my purse and head for the main entrance of One More Page. "Can you watch the store for an hour? I'm going home to change."

Mina ducks her head out from behind a shelf of books, a smile splitting her face. "Not until you tell me everything, and I mean *everything*."

Time to play the events of last night off as nothing because let's be honest, at the end of the day, that's all it was. An interesting way to pass the time.

Still, it sure rates higher than arguing or ignoring one another for twelve hours.

I shrug, digging for my keys in my bag to avoid Mina's heady stare. "Nothing to tell."

"Well, that's not true, is it?"

I raise my gaze and meet her smirk, a flush climbing my cheeks as she motions to my neck.

It's then I remember the souvenir Ash gifted me the night before. A souvenir I've half a mind to parade around his shop, just to watch the man squirm.

Petty? Absolutely, but I'm not too concerned with his

well-being at the moment. Especially not after I asked him out, and he shot me down.

He didn't even have the decency to agree to a date and then renege on it later. No, he flat out refused another go with me.

Bastard.

Mina strolls closer, her smile widening with each step. "And what a story you must have, my friend."

I huff out a breath and shake my head. "Don't start."

But Mina has no intention of letting this discussion lie. "Be sure to wear a turtleneck … unless you want to show off his handiwork to the world."

Mina means well, but I'm in no mood this morning.

"Is that a yes to watching the store?"

She shrugs, shoving a few books into their proper space on the shelf. "Is that a yes to telling me all the juicy details from last night?"

I rub my hand against my chin and bite back the rising frustration. "We survived, okay? End of story. Please don't ask me about it again."

The smile slides from Mina's face, replaced by a look of concern. She rarely sees this biting, dour side of me, and I can tell she's none too fond of it. "Are you okay? Did he do something to you?"

Where to begin.

But all I manage is a shake of my head, as the tears back up on me again. I need to leave now and collect myself.

Wash all reminders of Ash away.

I reach out and give Mina's hand a reassuring squeeze. "Don't mind me. I'm just grumpy from no sleep or coffee. Ash did nothing wrong. No worries there. I'll be back and get that damn window decorated. Otherwise, it might stand vacant until New Year's."

Of course, my friend knows I'm full of shit, but lucky for me, she lets the matter drop. "I'll get started on the window. Drive safe. It's icy out there."

Much like the interior of my heart now.

I force a smile and dash out the door. Only when I'm safe in my vehicle do I dare peer through the windows of Black Lotus, but there is no sign of their fearless leader anywhere.

No doubt he's well acquainted with the morning after walk of shame.

Then it hits me. How many other women have spent the night with Ash below our stores, snuggled together on that old couch?

Biting back the nausea, I shake my head, determined to clear it of any lingering thoughts of Asher Hammond.

Back to reality, and one thing is clear. His reality and my reality will never intersect, save for one night when I foolishly believed differently.

Chapter 9

The Trouble with Thorns

Ash

My eyes trail Ori's figure as she disappears up the stairs. When the now unlocked door closes behind her, I release a forceful sigh and scrub my face.

Talk about an unexpected turn of events.

I never, in a million years, thought Ori and I would end up as lovers.

Or that I would turn her down for a second round.

I hurt her with my response. I saw that mischievous, sexy as fuck light go out in her eyes and the mask she wears to protect herself from assholes like me slide into place.

She handled it well, pretending it didn't bother her to be just another night of fun—another notch on Asher Hammond's belt.

What did Ori tell me right before I made my move? She didn't want to be another name on my list, but I ensured she became one.

All because I can't allow any woman too close. Not even one as mesmerizing as Oriana Thorne.

At least I was on the level with her last night, telling her the bare, brutal truth about my theories of love and romance.

She knew.

Still doesn't negate one undisputed fact.

I. Am. An. Asshole.

With a grunt, I shove on my jeans and boots, rolling my neck to work out the kinks.

Back to my previously scheduled life.

My boots thud against the stairs, erasing any possibility of entering Black Lotus unseen. Wouldn't have mattered anyway, since both Braden and Zane are lounging on the reception area couch, wearing smug, matching, 'cat who ate the canary' grins when I walk in.

They plan on having a field day with this one.

I plan on cutting them off at the pass.

"Don't even say it," I warn, pointing at each of them in turn. "Not one fucking word."

Braden chuckles as he pulls out his phone to check the time. "I'm heading next door for some coffee. Unless you'd rather go in my stead, considering how you and Oriana have made up."

"Made up in all the right ways," Zane pipes in, earning a dark glower from me. "Don't deny it, man. You reek of sex."

It's hardly the first time I've done the deed without a shower to wash away the previous night's festivities, but somehow, Zane's words rub me the wrong way.

Especially when it comes to Ori.

I know he's pressing my buttons. Here's hoping he catches the energy wafting off me and stops. Immediately.

No such luck.

Zane snickers, resting his hands behind his head, a mocking grin on his face. "Those library types are always the wild ones. You'd never think it to look at her, but I guarantee that woman has some serious tricks up her sleeve."

"Watch your damn mouth," I mutter, fixing him with a no-holds-barred glare.

Zane's eyes widen at my tone, and he throws up his hands in surrender. "Shit. Take it easy. I didn't mean anything by it. Hell, the woman is gorgeous. If I had a chance to bang her—"

My hand reaches out to smack him against the back of his skull before my brain can even contemplate why. "I said, shut the fuck up about Ori."

"Leave it alone, Zane." As usual, Braden steps into his role as the official peacekeeper of the shop.

"Whatever," Zane replies, his mouth set in a tight line.

"Hey Ash," Braden says, pointing toward his office. "I need your opinion on my custom piece. Want to take a look?"

Cracking my knuckles, I roll my shoulders and follow Braden to the back of the shop, catching Zane's glower as I pass.

Once inside my brother's office, I collapse into a chair with a loud exhale.

"You okay?" Braden inquires, leaning against the desk.

I shrug. "Yeah. I'm fine."

Judging by his expression, my brother doesn't believe a word coming out of my mouth. "You sure about that? I know Zane's a little crass, but you don't normally take his head off like that."

I pinch the bridge of my nose, eyes squeezed shut as if that alone could stop the aggravation from spilling over. "I don't appreciate the shit Zane said about Ori. He doesn't know her."

"And you do?"

Must be my brother's turn to tread on thin ice.

"Not you too, man."

Braden shakes his head and gives me a light punch in the arm. "Nah, it's not my business, although Zane is right. Oriana is a beauty. Wicked smart, too."

Does he think I overlooked those parts of her after spending hours locked in her arms?

I scowl at Braden, but his grin only widens at my obvious discomfort over this topic.

Brothers. Can't live with 'em, illegal to bury them in a shallow, unmarked grave.

"Just saying. You could do way worse than a woman of that caliber."

"Nothing happened." I grit out the words, my patience at its end. If Braden refuses to change the direction of our conversation, I'll steer the train off the damn track.

Grabbing his tablet, I scan over the intricate floral and vine design.

Gotta hand it to my brother—he's a genius with floral blackwork shading.

"My client has real pale skin, so it's going to pop," Braden remarks.

I know someone else with pale skin. But she doesn't have any ink. I should know. I saw every inch of her last night.

She doesn't need it. Her body is its own work of art.

Every inch of Oriana Thorne is luscious fruit—delicious, tempting, and fucking forbidden after last night.

No matter how much my dick and mind hate the concept.

Braden nudges me, snapping me from my thoughts. "What do you think? Yes or no? It works, right?"

I toss down the tablet and release an aggravated grunt. "Will you stop asking about last night? There is nothing between Oriana and me. Case closed."

Braden grabs the tablet, closing out the drawing app. "I meant my design. But now I know where *your* head is at."

I SURVIVE ANOTHER FIFTEEN MINUTES BEFORE ORIANA ONCE again pervades my brain, dancing around my thoughts like a siren beckoning me to the depths.

Last night, I was eager and willing to drown just to make the moment last.

Here's the thing: I've had a lot of great sex. Copious amounts of between the sheets action. Gorgeous women of all ages and appearances. Utilized more positions and toys than a porn flick or sex store.

And I enjoy the hell out of sex. Sure, I've had some low points, but all together, it's been one crazy enjoyable ride.

Then there are my hours with Oriana.

When I was with her, nothing else existed. Nothing else mattered.

But there's no way, despite her pussy being the pinnacle of perfection, that it's affected me *this* much.

I'm working it up in my brain, making it bigger than it is.

Creating this narrative that fucking her was next level, voodoo shit that has turned me upside down.

Fucking. Love the term, hate it regarding Ori.

That's it. I have to lay eyes on her. Maybe then, in the light of morning, I'll see her for what she really is: a beautiful, smart woman who has given me the go-ahead on my speakeasy dream.

A friend who will celebrate the speakeasy's opening with a gratis cocktail.

Someone I can wave to and smile at when we pass on our way to separate lives.

Nothing more.

Then, I'll be able to stop fixating on last night.

Simple.

Scrubbing my face with my hands, I toss down my pencil and walk toward the front door.

All I need is some caffeine, a shower, and possibly a lobotomy.

"I'm getting some coffee next door. You want some, Zane?"

Yes, I make it a point to direct my question to him. It serves as my unofficial apology for being a dick earlier.

Zane shakes his head, his gaze intense as he dials in his tattoo machine, meticulously preparing for his next client. "I'm good."

That's a lie, if his short, clipped tone is anything to go by, and it's my fault for his bad mood this morning.

With a hard exhale, I close the distance between us. "Hey man, I'm sorry I lost it on you earlier. I just …"

But I don't finish my statement because, truthfully, I have no idea what to say. Myriads of emotions flood my mind, and I have zero idea what to do with any of them.

"It's cool, man." Zane looks up, a reassuring smile crossing his face. "We're good."

Just like that, our beef is forgotten.

If only the memory of Oriana Thorne's curves were that easy to erase.

Before I head to Ori's store, I duck downstairs and take a quick shower in the basement bathroom. It's in serious need of an upgrade, but at least it's this side of clean and the water pressure is good.

Besides, Zane mentioned I reek of sex, and I have a full day of clients. Despite my reputation, I prefer not to lead with that.

I pause for a moment outside the shower, the bar of soap and a shop towel in my hand. I still smell Ori on my skin, the faint hint of her moisturizer and heat.

Even hours later, she lingers there.

At least until I wash the last remnants of her away.

I need to get out of my head. Correction. I need to get *her* out of my head.

Hopefully, seeing her again will shake back into place all the shit that's now jangling around in my brain.

Twenty minutes later, I push open the door of One More Page, the bells jingling as I step across the threshold.

Sucking in a breath, I wait for the woman of the hour to appear.

No such luck, as Mina pokes her head out from behind a bookshelf and shoots me a coy grin. "Asher Hammond."

"Morning, Mina."

The willowy blonde walks toward me, and I give her an appreciative once-over. She's a beauty—a true California girl who's never set foot in California.

But despite Mina's obvious good looks, she doesn't do it for me.

One, because I know Braden has a thing for her, although he will never admit that fact. Per him, she's too young. Too innocent. And *that* is too much of a dangerous combination.

But I also know my brother has banged women far younger than Mina. Hell, she's twenty-five, not eighteen.

But the real reason her long and lean looks don't do it for me?

I've recently come to realize that I have a type.

A particular kind of woman who makes me weak in the knees and causes my heart to do things no heart should ever do. A woman who takes my breath away and occupies my every thought.

A woman I can't allow myself to go near again.

And that's a fact I must keep reminding myself.

Every damn second.

"Two days in a row. That's a new record. Cup of joe for you?" Mina asks, arching one well-manicured brow at me before heading toward the coffee bar.

It's hard to determine if the woman is digging for information, but for now, I opt to play it off.

"I hear you serve the best coffee in town."

"Among other things. I'm surprised to see you here again so soon. Out of character for you. Or is this your new normal?"

Her wink solidifies it.

She suspects something. Now, to determine how much and in what detail.

Hey, women talk about this kind of crap. I know, because I'm often the topic of conversation where the women of this town are concerned.

I tug a hand through my hair and chuckle. "You caught me. I have an ulterior motive this morning."

"Knew it." She bites her lower lip to keep from laughing, but her eyes dance with amusement.

Sorry, kid. I'm not caving that easily.

"I need some books on the Roaring '20s. Topics like architecture, fashion, food. That sort of thing. I figured you fine ladies would be the people to ask."

Mina nods, the sarcastic gleam falling from her eyes. "Oh, I assumed you were here to visit with Ori. Guess she signed the paperwork for you?"

I rock back on my heels and shove my hands in my pockets, feeling the heat rise in my cheeks.

What the fuck is wrong with me? Now I can't hold up my end of a basic conversation with a woman I *don't* want to sleep with?

"Well, not yet, but she's agreed to the idea. I've been dreaming about this for a long time, so I want to dive in right away. Why wait, right?"

"I can't wait to see what you come up with. It's going to be so much fun." Mina hands me a cup of coffee and motions to the far side of the store. "Grab a seat and I'll look. See what I can find."

I relax into a buttery soft leather armchair and take a swig of the coffee.

Braden was right. Best damn coffee in town.

A few customers mill around the store, browsing the

racks of books, while soft jazz flows out of the speakers and a fire crackles warmly from the stove in the reading nook.

I get it now. There is a comfort and warmth within these walls, a haven from the busy and often blustery world.

Then again, knowing the owner, I'm not surprised.

Oriana Thorne is a glowing fire after a hard day.

Once again, I'm thinking about her.

I grab a hardcover off the table and peruse the pages. It's about local legends, and trust me, there are tons of ghost stories in these mountains.

I should know. My life is one of them, and not because of encounters with the spirit world.

My ghost prefers a different type of haunting, taking up residence in my soul and ensuring no one else stands a chance.

Her name is Lucille, and her presence is everywhere, permeating all the layers of my heart and reminding me what happens when you dare to love someone that much.

After she ripped my world apart ten years ago, I mired in self-loathing for a while, until my friends grabbed me by the collar and talked some sense into me.

They reminded me of her flawed character and questionable past, all things I overlooked because of my hopeless adoration.

To them, Lucille was like a bad case of fleas who needed to be shaken off without a second glance. Then, I needed to move on and live my best life—the ultimate payback.

Somehow, I don't think my morphing into the town player is *quite* what they had in mind.

But I'm happy and I am living my best life.

I don't need one woman by my side when I have a line of them waiting for their chance.

Variety is the spice of life, right?

Plus, when you don't get attached emotionally, you're safe. Getting your heart smashed is not something I recommend, especially not when it can be just as easily avoided.

Lucille ripped my soul to shreds and no matter how much I'd love to forget that massacre, it's burned into my brain.

Etched like a tattoo, a permanent reminder of that one time, I led with my heart and left a fool.

I'll never tread that path again. Not for any woman.

Mina perches on the couch across from me, placing several books on the oak coffee table. "We don't have anything specific to speakeasies, but I'm sure we can order something. These books delve into the '20s as a whole, covering everything from architecture to Prohibition. Maybe you can glean something from them."

"This is a good start. Thanks." I flip through the pages of one book, chancing a few glances toward the back of the store.

I know Ori's office is back there, which means *she's* likely back there. Avoiding me.

I fucking hate that idea.

Mina returns with a laptop in her arms and shows me the screen. "Check this out. It covers Art Deco design, and the lost art of the speakeasy."

"It's perfect. Damn, you're good."

"Wasn't me. Ori found it."

So, she *is* here, which means she's definitely avoiding me.

Mina, oblivious to my inner monologue, prattles on

about the topics covered in the book. All I can manage is a forced smile, my gaze drifting repeatedly to the back of the store.

After last night, she's going to pretend she doesn't know me? What nonsense is that?

Then it hits me.

It's the exact same nonsense I've been telling myself all morning. Only difference? I'm not used to being on this side of the situation and I can say without a doubt, I don't like it here.

"Ori is a regular guru with research," Mina explains, chuckling as she types into the laptop. "Give that woman any topic and she'll return with piles of information. Anyway, she told me to order it for the store. You can browse through it whenever you like."

I tear my gaze from the rear of the store and send Mina a wink. "Knew I'd come to the right place."

Mina nods, her gaze on the screen. "We're pretty accommodating here."

"So Braden tells me."

Now it's *my* turn to bite back a laugh at the pink flush spreading across Mina's cheeks.

Damn, she's got it bad.

And for her, that ain't good.

"I'm glad he approves. He's generally so quiet in here," Mina stammers.

Probably because you make him nervous, too.

I shake my head and take another swig of coffee. "Braden is shy. Shyer than me, anyway. But he's a damn good man."

Bragging on my brother isn't a rarity, although I hope Mina doesn't catch on to the fact that I'm prolonging this conversation, and it has *nothing* to do with her crush on Braden.

She fixes me with her light blue gaze. "He always said the same thing about you, but until recently, Ori held a far different opinion."

I snort, running a hand over my jaw. "Glad I could convince her otherwise."

Mina crosses her arms tightly over her chest, her eyes narrowing as she holds my gaze. "I bet you did."

Shit. Time to backtrack.

"That is not how I meant it. I'm glad Ori is on my side now, or I'm on hers. We're on the same side."

Now I'm babbling like a moron.

Judging by Mina's stilted expression, she isn't buying what I'm selling.

I take pride in being one of the good guys in Sparkwood, but recent events make me wonder about the truth in that claim.

Seems the first thing people assume when they see me is how I'm a good-looking good time. One who has been sampled by countless women, with countless more in the wings.

A shallow facade covering a broken and dark pool where no one dares to tread. Mainly because I deny everyone entrance.

I damn near let Ori in last night. There was a moment after our third round, where she drifted off against my chest. She lay there, so warm against my skin, her breathing soft and even.

I stroked her hair, dropping kisses to the sweet-scented strands, and imagined a moment, decades from now, where we lay together just like this. After years of love, arguments, the highs and lows of life, we still found peace in each other's arms.

I only allowed it to linger a few seconds, but for that brief instant, I felt whole again.

Or I just read into something that wasn't there, much like I did with Lucille.

Tossing the book on the table, I crack my knuckles and steal another glance down the darkened back hallway of the bookstore.

"She's not back there," Mina states, her mouth a thin line.

So much for flying under the radar.

"You mean Ori?"

Mina scoffs and wags her finger at me. "Yes. The woman you've been looking for this entire time."

Silence fills the space between Mina and me as her words settle over me like a blanket.

The woman I've been looking for this entire time.

What the hell is wrong with everyone this morning? Seems the staff of both shops are determined to marry me off to the petite bookstore owner.

Well, they need to settle down. Ori and I spent one night together. It hardly qualifies as marriage material.

"Did Ori say something happened between us?"

Mina shakes her head. "Not a word, but there was that unfortunate incident with the vacuum cleaner. What else could leave such a mark on her neck, right?"

I sputter my coffee, earning a wicked grin from Mina as I recall the hickey I gifted Ori the night before. "Shit. Forgot about that. Did you mention it to her?"

"Kind of hard to ignore, considering it was front and

center on Ori's throat. She grabbed her purse and bolted home to change into a turtleneck. Damn vacuums."

I glide my tongue ring along my lower lip, chuckling. "Vacuums are known to possess a fierce temperament at times."

"Hopefully it will fade away before any of her dates take notice."

What the hell?

I cut my gaze from the far wall to Mina's face, trying to gauge if she's serious with that statement. "I didn't think she was dating anyone."

"She's not, but there have been plenty of men asking her out. Can you blame them?"

Okay, she's baiting me and damn it all, it's working. I tap my boot along the floor as the aggravation flows through my body.

Time to slide on my 'I don't give a fuck' face. After all, it's not like *my* bed has been cold.

"Can't blame them at all. She's one hell of a woman."

"Not the love 'em and leave 'em type, though. Ori is a real romantic. A firm believer in true love and happily ever after. Just waiting for the right guy to come along and sweep her off her feet."

"Look—"

Mina waves her hand, dismissing whatever cockamamie excuse I planned to employ. "Heavens, I didn't mean *you*. Ori isn't your type. Not your style. Not your vibe. I know that, and so does she. It's your loss, though, because the woman is fabulous."

Tell me something I don't know.

Mina stacks the books in a neat pile, smiling at a

customer when they enter. "Besides, you're not her type, either."

Time for me to leave because now my temper wants a piece of the action.

I sure as hell was Ori's type last night.

And she was my every fantasy come to life.

Grabbing my coffee, I stand up and offer Mina a mock salute. "I'd better get back, but thanks for ordering that book. Let me know it comes in."

"Will do. See you guys at the festival."

Thank God. A truly benign topic.

Our holiday festival is an outdoor street fair hosted every year by the powers that be in Sparkwood. Yes, outdoors. In winter. In upstate New York.

While the residents of Sparkwood know how to have fun, no one ever accused us of possessing a lick of common sense.

"Absolutely. Wouldn't miss that tradition."

Mina grins at me. "Ori thinks we're all nuts for hosting a festival outside in the freezing cold."

"Maybe we can convince her otherwise."

"Maybe *you* have a better chance of that," Mina replies, her eyes crinkling with thinly veiled amusement. "I have to ring up a customer."

Do I let Mina have the last word? Yes, because if she's anything like her boss, she's got an arsenal of comebacks at the ready.

Of course, no one has a mouth like Oriana Thorne.

No one.

For the first time, I leave One More Page as a friend. This concept should reassure me, but I'm more confused than ever as questions swirl in my brain.

How many men have asked Ori out? How many offers has she accepted? How long until a man does swoop in and yank her from the market?

And why the fuck do I care so much?

I replay last night's events over and over until I'm so tangled up in emotions that I'm tempted to pick the lock to Ori's office and await her return.

Then, I'll take exactly thirty seconds to sink inside her and finish what my brother interrupted this morning.

Not her type, my ass. I'll make her beg for more, all the while screaming my name.

Leave it alone, Ash. Better yet, leave her alone.

Yep, that's the safe option.

And yet, it feels like the worst choice imaginable.

Chapter 10

Burning Boundaries

Ash

"Sign there and there." Kiki slides the paperwork across the table to me, motioning to the two lines requiring my signature.

A new lease, allowing me to move ahead with my speakeasy plans.

I scan the agreement, noting Ori's signature already in place. Her penmanship is feminine but with a quiet power. A surety in every stroke.

Delicate but deliciously dangerous.

Much like the woman herself.

And there goes my brain again, traveling the same path it's been on since yesterday.

"She already signed? That was quick."

Kiki offers me a blasé shrug. "Goes to show the strength of your charm when you aim it properly."

Somehow, I doubt that's the reason, but I'm thrilled Ori didn't renege on her agreement after our stilted goodbye yesterday morning. Or, should I say, *my* stilted goodbye.

She caught me off guard with the dinner offer and

although I'd love to sample her wares daily, it's not a good idea.

For either of us.

Will I continue feeding myself these mental lines of bullshit? Until they push me into the grave.

I fell prey to a woman once. There won't be a sequel.

"Done and done," I reply, setting the pen down with a satisfied flourish next to my newly revised lease agreement.

Kiki nods and smiles before slipping the paperwork into her briefcase. "Congratulations, Ash. I can't wait to sample a cocktail in your new speakeasy."

I lean against the pub booth with a relieved sigh and hold up my glass of whiskey for a toast. "That's still a few months off, but at least I've cleared one obstacle."

Kiki clinks my glass with her own before taking a sip. "So, is Oriana Thorne still a wretched bog witch?"

I stare at my drink but can't hold back the smile splitting my face. "Not even close."

"Told you."

"You were right," I concede, eager to steer the conversation away from the petite, elusive bookstore owner who has effectively avoided me the past two days.

No joke, she always seemed to be *just* out of sight when I passed by or stopped in for my second, third, and fourth cup of coffee.

Hey, I didn't get much sleep the other night—or last night, if we're being honest. No, my brain kept me awake into the wee hours, ruminating on Oriana Thorne.

After two nights with barely any shuteye, I needed copious amounts of caffeine.

Nothing more to it than that.

But Kiki is not content to let the subject lie. Figures.

"I have to ask. How did you manage it?"

I shoot her a wink and take another swallow from my glass. "With that wicked charm you claim I have in spades."

Kiki snorts out a laugh and buries her face in her hand. "Why am I not surprised?"

"A locked basement door didn't hurt the cause, either."

My friend quirks her brow at me, my words catching her unaware. "You and Ori got locked in the basement?"

"Yep."

She runs her fingers along the edge of her glass, and I can't tell if she approves or thinks I'm out of my damn mind. "Was that gravity's fault or yours?"

I chuckle, taking another sip of my whiskey. "Gravity, obviously."

"Bullshit."

I lean forward, resting my hands on the table. "Fine. It was intentional, but necessary. I needed ample time to chip away at Ori's preconceived notions about me."

"How long were you stuck down there?"

I drag my tongue against my lower lip as a vision of Ori spread out beneath me once again enters my brain. "All night long."

"Did you two have fun?"

I dust my knuckles along my jacket and blow on them. "She signed the new lease, didn't she?"

Kiki clicks her tongue against her teeth, her nails tapping the wood table in an aggravated rhythm. My old friend is about to serve me a stern lecture on the accouterments of love and romance. "You know I love you, right?"

God, this is about to get painful. "Yep."

"But I *hate* the way you live your life. Are you honestly happy dating a different woman every damn day?"

"Are you seriously asking me that question? Don't most men love that lifestyle?"

Kiki drops her head to her hand and huffs out a breath. "Not most men, no. Most men, like most women, like the idea of falling in love and settling down. You won't even entertain the concept."

"Different strokes, right? I'm not one of those guys."

"Because you don't give it a chance. Look, I accepted the idea of casual dating when you and I were together, but not because I didn't want more. With you, there was no other option."

What the hell? Please don't tell me my former fuck buddy is rekindling feelings for me. Especially not when her husband is also my friend and the local chief of police.

That is a migraine I do *not* need.

"Kiki—"

She waves her hands, silencing me. "Shelve your ego, Ash. I've been over you for years. After I met Drake, there was no going back. He offered me everything you wouldn't give me. No questions asked."

"If you recall, I introduced you to Drake, so I'm thrilled it worked out."

And I am glad. Even though I'm a confirmed bachelor, I never begrudge my bedmates when they find their forever person. Do some hope I might be that guy? Sure, most do. But they quickly realize I mean what I say about love.

We don't mix.

Period. End of story.

Besides, love isn't meant for everyone.

Case in point, me.

"Is there a point to this lecture or are you just crapping

all over my buzz?" I ask, quirking an eyebrow at my former fling as I lean back against the wooden booth.

"Mark my words: one day, you'll meet a woman who will turn you on your head. You won't be able to stop thinking about her and all those claims about hating love will up and vanish. Then you'll join the rest of us lovesick fools in that magical fairytale place known as wedded bliss."

I roll my eyes and bark out a laugh. "Not a chance in hell. Don't you know me by now?"

Kiki throws up her hands. "Fine. Maybe I'm wrong and you'll continue to bed the local female population of Sparkwood until your dying day."

Now we're talking. "There are worse ways to go."

Do I sound like a heartless prick? Without a doubt, but I'll do anything to change the path of this conversation.

Kiki glances over my shoulder, her lips curling into a smile. "Well, well. Speak of the devil. Look who's here."

When I turn, I half expect to see any number of my recent conquests huddled by the entrance, glowers on their faces as they demand to know why I despise the idea of love.

But no, it's her. The siren herself—Oriana Thorne.

My pulse spikes as my gaze moves over her slight form, knowing all too well what lays hidden beneath her trench coat.

Suddenly, it's a thousand degrees in here and I drag a hand across my brow before shrugging off my jacket.

Maybe I'm allergic to the woman, considering the effect she's having on me.

Yeah, that's got to be it.

"Oriana," Kiki calls out, waving her over, before shooting me a dagger-edged glance. "Be nice."

"Yes, ma'am," I retort, a snort of indignation escaping my throat.

What the hell does Kiki think I'll do? Berate the woman for letting me have my way? Perhaps pounce on her after she signed the new lease?

Although, that second option sounds damn good. Ori claimed to have joined the mile high club. Perhaps I can convince her to sample a few more public places.

Check off some boxes on both our lists.

Jesus Christ, I'm a fucking disaster. I can't go two minutes without picturing myself buried inside Ori's heat.

Her warm, tight, wet pussy.

"Hi Kiki."

Just those two words from Ori's delectable mouth are all I need to hear. Her smooth voice, like honied velvet, washes over me, reminding me of all the deliciously dirty things she whispered the night before, when she unraveled me with her words and every exquisite curve.

Now, it's my turn to return the favor.

Ori refocuses her gaze as those big brown eyes lock onto me. "Hello, Ash."

I lean back against the booth, letting the wood press into my shoulders as I drape my arms along the top, the fabric of my shirt stretching across my well-developed pecs.

Is it an intentional move? Absolutely.

A smirk tugs at the corner of my mouth when I spy the turtleneck she's sporting—pulled all the way up to her jaw. "Nice sweater."

A flush climbs her cheeks as she averts her gaze. "Good for keeping me warm when it's positively frigid outside."

"I know a few other things that might work even better."

She catches her lower lip between her teeth as that mischievous gleam enters her eyes.

Game on.

"I'm sure you're an expert in that field." Ori shifts her weight, her fingers pulling at the neckline of her sweater. Yep, I'm getting to her and I'm loving every damn second.

"Careful, Little One. You don't want to accidentally show off whatever it is you're hiding." Then I lean forward, resting my elbows on the table, my gaze never faltering from her face.

She laughs, and it upends me, just like it did the other night. When she meets my lingering stare, I see the desire flickering in her face. She's reliving the same memories I am, and it's having the same heated effect. "I have *no* idea what you're talking about."

Tilting my head, I motion toward her sweater. "Need me to remind you?"

"Do you two need a minute?" Kiki interjects.

When I swing my head to look at my friend, I catch her amused smile.

Shit. I forgot she was sitting there.

Once again, I got totally lost in Oriana.

Talk about some powerful magic.

"What?" I manage.

Kiki wags her finger between Ori and me. "You two. Seems you have important topics to discuss. Do you need some privacy, or would you prefer I continue to pose as a voyeur?"

My former fuck buddy is having way too much fun at my expense.

I push myself from the booth and jerk my thumb

toward the bar. "Actually, I need another drink. Ori, what's your poison?"

"Nothing for me."

"Not even a glass of single malt?" I tease.

"Not tonight. I'm just here to grab some food."

Kiki pats the seat next to her. "Sit down and Ash will get the server over here. We were just discussing his new venture. Thanks to you, it's a go for liftoff."

Ori shoots Kiki a smile. "Happy to be of service. I'd love to join you, but my food is almost ready. We ordered it to-go."

I stiffen when I catch her words. *We?* Who exactly are *we?*

I don't wait long for an answer.

"Got our food. You ready to head home, Ori?"

A male voice steps uninvited into our conversation, and I cut my gaze toward him as one thought shoots through my mind.

Who the fuck is this?

This guy's got the whole professor vibe going—tweed jacket, glasses perched on his nose, and not a hair out of place. An Ivy League prep who likely has a deluge of initials after his name.

I hate him immediately.

Kiki extends her hand to the man while shooting me a coy side-eye. "Hi, there. I'm Kiki, the local realtor."

Ori motions to the man at her side—a man standing entirely too close for my liking. "This is Roger. We worked together in the city."

Which doesn't explain what Professor Plaid Patches is doing here now. We're ninety minutes outside of Manhattan.

Far too many miles to travel for a bite to eat.

No, this is an intentional visit and judging by the looks he's shooting at Ori, he has plans for an all-night party.

I shake his hand, ensuring I employ my tightest 'don't fuck with me' grip. "Asher Hammond."

When he winces, I know I've done my job. "Hell of a grip," he says, adjusting his glasses.

Buddy, that isn't all I have.

Instead, I shrug and grunt. That's about as friendly as I can manage right now.

"Here you go, handsome," a voice says at my elbow. "I saw you were running on empty."

Talk about perfect timing. I pivot toward the striking bartender, offering her my signature smile as I accept a fresh glass of whiskey. "You know me too well."

"Actually, I don't know you well enough," she replies with a wink, planting her hand on her hip.

It's an overt gesture, but I love her for it, even though I don't know the bartender's name and haven't given her a speck of attention until now.

All Oriana will see is a beautiful woman coming onto me. Will I play that to my advantage? Damn right, I will.

"We'll have to work on that, won't we?" I pull a twenty from my wallet and tuck it into her front pocket, watching her eyes alight.

See, Oriana? You're not the only one who's moved on.

"We will. Come find me when you're done." With a final hip shake, the bartender returns to her post, and I cross my arms triumphantly over my chest and shoot a cocky grin toward Oriana.

Judging by the tight set of her jaw, she is *not* amused.

Join the club. Besides, she started it with Mr. Plaid

Patches Yale wannabe. No way in hell that man can fuck worth a damn. No one wearing elbow patches knows how to please a woman.

But I sure as hell do, and now I have a very interested party to spend the evening with.

Game over. I win.

"We'd better go," Ori's schmuck says, giving her sleeve a gentle tug. "Don't want our food to get cold."

Ori nods, but the aggravation is still clear on her face. "Absolutely. Have a good night."

She reaches over, giving Kiki a hug. Then, in a totally unexpected move, she turns to me and opens her arms. "Don't worry if she sees you. Your bartender friend doesn't seem the type to be easily dissuaded. Besides, I've earned a hug."

Before I can respond, Ori steps in closer, wrapping her arms around my waist. My breath catches as her body presses into mine with a warmth that sends a jolt of memory through me.

Her cheek rests against my chest, and for a moment, I feel her breathing in sync with mine. I fold her into my embrace, ducking my head to breathe in the sweet scent of her hair—a scent that is uniquely hers.

"Congratulations. I'm really happy for you," she murmurs.

I slide a finger under her chin, forcing her eyes to meet mine. "All because of you."

She starts to pull back, her body instinctively trying to create distance, but I'm not ready to let her go. My grip tightens, just enough to keep her close, to make her under-stand there's still something unfinished between us.

I lower my head, brushing my mouth against hers in the

lightest, softest kiss—a mere whisper of contact. It's barely there, yet the weight of it lingers in the air, saying everything we haven't. Her breath hitches, and I can't resist leaning in further, my lips grazing the shell of her ear as I murmur, "He's not what you need."

Ori bites her lip, her eyes flickering with amusement. A small chuckle escapes on a sigh, tinged with irony. "Neither is she, and we both know it."

Her words hang in the air between us, undeniable and sharp, cutting through whatever game we're playing. For all my bravado, she sees right through me, and she isn't afraid to call me out on the fact.

She breaks free from my grip and offers a last smile before linking arms with Professor Prep and walking out the door.

Fucking hell.

Do I want to stop Ori from leaving? Of course, but then what? Demand her time and energy, only to shove her away again tomorrow?

One night. That was the agreement. At least on my end.

I can't be angry she's abiding by it.

That's what my head says. My fists want to pummel that preppy bastard into the ground.

Releasing a low growl, I swig back half my drink, slamming the glass on the table as I sit down.

Then I notice Kiki's bemused expression.

"What?" I snap.

"You tell me."

I yank a hand through my hair and heave out a sigh. "You know, I get called Mr. One Night Stand all the time, yet here she is, not forty-eight hours later, with another guy, and it's fine."

Now Kiki's grin is full-fledged.

"What is so damn funny?"

"That woman I mentioned earlier? The one who would turn you upside down? Looks like you've already met her."

"Who? Ori? No. Not at all."

"Right. Not even a little bit." She shrugs with a knowing smirk. "I guess she isn't your type, though."

What is it with women and that line?

Is there a handbook somewhere that describes my perfect woman?

One that states a gorgeous, sexy as fuck librarian type couldn't possibly fit the bill for me? Because I'd like to see it, and then burn the damn thing.

"Exactly." I mumble the words, knowing it's total crap, before flagging the bartender for another refill. The whiskey is going down way too easily now, and for all the wrong reasons. The gorgeous redhead smiles in my direction and sets about making my drink. "She'll do nicely, though."

Kiki glances at the bartender and shakes her head. "She won't cure what ails you, although it's likely a good thing you have a backup plan, all things considered."

"Considering what?"

"Ori's date for the evening."

Kiki is pushing all my buttons right now. I'm not sure what she hopes to accomplish, outside of pushing my anger into the red.

Drumming an erratic rhythm against the table with my fingers, I will myself to relax.

I'm fully aware the women I bed take other lovers, and

vice versa. We're adults having a good time. It's not serious and so long as we're safe and honest, it's not a problem.

That is *not* the case with Ori's buddy from Manhattan.

Him, I want to dismember and bury in a shallow grave.

And Kiki knows it—relishing every second as she watches me squirm.

"I better go." Kiki stands up and pulls her coat off the hook at the end of the booth. "I have to admit, it's nice to see."

"See what?"

"You, all tangled up over Oriana Thorne."

I roll my eyes before giving her a kiss on the cheek. "Be safe driving. Give Drake my best."

Then she's gone into the night, heading toward her cozy house where her husband awaits her arrival.

I'm glad for her. Truly.

But that Oriana is also warm and cozy tonight and it's *not* with me?

Not so much.

The sexy redhead delivers me a fresh drink and I notice I'm the only one getting this level of personal service—not that I'm complaining. "Hey Ash, why don't you come join me at the bar? I'll be off in an hour and then you and I can have some fun."

No doubt she'll be a hell of a good time, too.

Only trouble with that scenario? I don't want her in my bed.

I want the tiny brunette who left not ten minutes ago with some preppy schlep who doesn't deserve her.

"Sorry, love, but I'm calling it a night."

"What about your drink?"

I push a fifty into her hand. "For your trouble."

The bartender's face falls, but she covers it with a practiced smile. "Another time, then."

I nod and grab my coat, heading for my bike.

In truth, I have a thumping headache and neither another drink nor a roll in the hay with that cutie will help.

As I ease onto the street and head towards my farm, I allow my thoughts to drift back to my night with Ori. But I'm not thinking about the sex, even though it was spectacular.

Instead, I ruminate on her laugh as she told me a silly story about her childhood and how fucking pretty she looked.

Understatement of the century.

Oriana is gorgeous in every sense of the word. Besides her outward beauty, she's fiercely intelligent, possessing an impressive array of street skills for such a bookish type. But it's that vulnerable underbelly, caught in a few brief instances, that threatens to undo me.

I want to know all those moments, but that means a whole new set of rules for me.

And that? That I can't allow.

Chapter 11

The Frost Queen's Undoing

Ori

"Excuse me, can I borrow your bathroom?"

I glance up from my work, forcing a smile for the scantily clad woman hovering by my office door. "Promise to bring it back?"

She furrows her brow as my witty retort flies straight over her head. "What?"

I wave my hand and bite back a laugh. "Go ahead. Last door on the left."

"Thanks." She mumbles her reply while adjusting her top, shooting wary glances toward the skimpy fabric to confirm its placement.

Might as well ask the obvious question.

"Aren't you cold?"

It's a legitimate inquiry, considering she's wearing a bustier with no coat and it's barely 35 degrees outside. When you add in the wind chill, it's arctic level.

"Freezing, but I want to look good."

"I suppose you mean for the holiday fair?"

And I know she doesn't give a rat's ass about looking good for *my* benefit.

Her focus is entirely on the men of Black Lotus, who are currently ensconced in the parking lot beneath a massive black tent—complete with a heater, alcohol, and a bevy of women.

Of course, maybe she's set her sights on Braden or Zane. They're both wildly handsome. It's not like *every* woman has a thing for Asher Hammond.

The busty blonde nods, glancing towards Main Street. "I got here early. Had to beat the rush. You know how women are around him."

I click my tongue against my teeth and roll my eyes. I can continue this farce, but what's the point? "Women love Ash, and he loves them."

"Exactly." She straightens, adjusting her top once more. "How do I look?"

Fucking ridiculous.

But I bite my tongue and force a smile in the young woman's direction. "Hot as hell. No doubt you'll catch Ash's attention dressed like that."

She releases a sated breath. "Perfect. Thank you. See you outside."

"Can't wait," I mutter as she heads for the bathroom, her heels tapping against the hardwood floor.

The truth is, I have zero desire to attend this street fair. Call me a hothouse flower, but my options for the day are either freezing my tits off in the cold or seeking out the warmth in Black Lotus's tent—while witnessing Ash's flirtations with his harem.

A tricky decision.

One that Mina has apparently made for me as she

pokes her head into my office. "Come on, it's time to make an appearance."

"Do I have to?" Yes, I'm whining.

"For a little bit, at least."

"But we have an entire setup inside the store, where it's warm. Why should I traverse outside when my customers are already inside?"

"Tradition."

Desperate times call for desperate measures. Time to break out the theatrics.

I heave a dramatic sigh, slumping over my desk as if the mere idea of this excursion has drained the life from me. "I'm not equipped for this level of cold. It's inhumane."

Mina walks across my office, patting my head like a spoiled dog. "Poor little city girl. You'll manage. Besides, the guys were asking where you were."

"What guys?" I mutter, my head still hiding in my arms.

"The hotties from Black Lotus, that's who."

I tip my head up, resting my chin on my hand. "I highly doubt they care."

Mina shrugs, grabs my coat off the corner rack, and deposits it on my desk. "Ash seemed real interested in why you were still holed up in here."

Now I know she's lying.

Ash and I haven't spoken since that night at the bar, when he flirted openly with another woman right before kissing me and intimating that my friend Roger couldn't satisfy my needs.

Since Roger is happily married to James, I'm inclined to agree with him.

I wonder if Ash took that redheaded bartender up on

her offer after I left. My money is on yes, although Mina finds the entire situation adorable.

After telling her the details of that run-in, she declared Ash was jealous, and that precipitated his behavior. Why else would he have kissed me in plain view of his next conquest?

My response to her absurd idea? Ash enjoys toying with women, and at this point, I'm just one of many—a footnote in his massive black book. Hell, it's more than a book. It's a damn encyclopedia.

Sure, the war between the shops is over, and there's a noticeable change in the atmosphere, at least for our employees. Ash drops into the store daily, but he never lingers. He grabs his coffee, shoots me a wink and a wave, then returns next door.

That's the extent of our relationship—or whatever you call it.

It seems the man maintains a tight schedule, and there simply isn't room in it for me.

Not that I care … or am counting how many days it's been since our fateful night together in the basement.

"I've got an idea," I exclaim, rubbing my hands together. "I'll give you the rest of the afternoon off so you can hang out with the guys. Spend time with Braden. I'll stay here and manage the store."

For a second, I think my plan might convince her, but one look at Mina's exasperated face and I have my answer.

Not happening.

With a huff, I close my laptop and start layering for the weather. Unlike Ash's fan club, I won't risk frostbite.

I yank the scarf from its hook, wrapping it tightly around my neck—more to vent my irritation than to ward off the cold. Then I snatch up the hat and jam it onto my head. Finally, I grab my trench coat, shrugging into it with sharp, jerky movements.

"Let's get this over with," I grumble, as I trail Mina through our store and out into the parking lot.

Don't get me wrong, I adore the holiday season. I'm a nut for festivities and all the trappings related to Christmas. What I'm *not* a fan of is pretending to be disinterested in front of Sparkwood's resident bad boy.

So far, it's been a non-issue, since I've barely seen Asher in the last few days. I can pretend he, and our fun-filled romp, are only figments of my imagination.

But now, that figment is live and in color and I am so unprepared for this moment.

My sole armor for this battle is sarcasm—the biting edge of my personality that serves to protect my heart from utter decimation.

Not that Ash has my heart by any stretch, because that would be a stupid and pointless endeavor.

Right?

But my crisis with Ash is momentarily forgotten when I step into Sparkwood's winter wonderland. I'll give it to the locals—they know how to throw a party—even if frostbite is a side effect of attendance.

Up and down Main Street stands a bevy of tents and carts, each one offering local fare and crafts. Lights hang on everything from lampposts to awnings and fire pits burn in the middle of the street, offering a warm reprieve from winter's chill.

The aroma of gingerbread and mulled wine dance across the air, and my stomach rumbles in response.

"Pretty, right?" Mina asks, waving at a few patrons as they stroll by, their arms laden with packages.

"Beautiful. A storybook come to life."

Hell, even the men from Black Lotus have joined in on the festivities, although their tent decor leans more toward gothic Dickens than Santa's workshop.

Mina and I enter the tented area, and I realize if Ash's speakeasy looks anything like the interior of this temporary hangout, he'll have an instant hit on his hands.

Velvet drapes hang along the walls, helping to block the chill while providing a holiday aesthetic and battery-operated lanterns flicker throughout the area. A small bar sits in the back corner, next to a portable photo booth.

Judging by the dozen or so women hanging out in the tent, Ash also brought along his collection of fuck buddies.

Or at least this week's installment.

I sound like a bitter hag. The embodiment of the crotchety old maid Ash believed me to be—at least until I proved I can also deliver one hell of a good time.

A good time Ash never wants to experience again. At least, not with me.

Why would he? The man got his wish—my signature on our newly revised deed.

Although Mina disputes my theory, I reckon that was Ash's intention all along. Butter me up, rub me down, hand me the pen, and duck out the door with nary a backward glance.

Well played, Asher Hammond. Well played.

Still, I can't hate the man for using his talents to his advantage. Isn't that what we all do? And he never lied about his intentions with me. Ash promised to love the fuck out of me that night and he made good on his threat.

I just wish I could write off the evening as easily as he did.

But, until I reach that juncture, I need to fake it.

How hard can it be?

Glancing around the tent's interior, I realize the woman in my store earlier was overdressed. Some of these chicks are wearing little more than lingerie.

Each one is pretty and playing up their assets to the fullest, so there is *no* mistaking their intention.

Right in the middle of the melee stands the man they've all come to see—Asher Hammond.

He's casually dressed in a leather jacket and jeans, every inch of him epitomizing the quintessential heartbreaker.

Every move, gesture, and smile from the angelic bad boy oozes charm. He's effortless.

I hate him for it.

Then there's me, on the opposite side of the social spectrum. Stilted and painfully awkward, I lack Ash's finesse with crowds.

Small groups are where I shine, but when there's too much noise from too many people, my introverted nature kicks into high gear and I fade into the wallpaper. Or, in this case, the velvet drapes.

Trust me, it's better for everyone that way.

But as I watch the women flirt and giggle with Ash, I wish I had a bit more moxie at my disposal.

Then again, I've never been one to fish for attention, especially not where men are concerned. Way too much upkeep with that crown. And judging by the flock gathered around the man of the hour, that crown has several ladies-in-waiting.

Men are either interested in me, or they're not, and I

refuse to ply them with fake charm and empty flattery to sway their favor.

Seems I'm in the minority where Asher Hammond is concerned.

"He's popular," Mina observes, giving me a light jab in the ribs.

Understatement of the month right there.

"Tell me something we don't know."

"I know someone who knows *way* more about him than any of these women." Mina shoots me a smirk, her eyes gleaming with mischief.

Subtle, love. Subtle.

She'd love for me to cave and provide her with every intimate detail of my night with Ash, but what's the point? Although I may know him on a deeper level than his current flock, there are a ton of other women who share the same notation on their resume.

I cringe to think how many women Asher Hammond has bedded in his thirty-eight years, or what his final tally will be once his ride on earth is done.

Although, his rampant sexual history is apparently a non-issue with his fan base. He never denies who or what he is, and more importantly, what he isn't.

Maybe that's the trick: Ash tells his bed buddies the truth right off the bat so they can't throw it in his face later. Brilliant chess move.

I still hate him for it … even though I don't hate him at all.

A thin brunette takes her turn with the man of the hour, lifting her skirt to show off a large floral piece tattooed on her upper thigh.

Ash squats down before her, his fingers tracing delicately over the inked outline, but it's the look on the woman's face when he touches her that catches my attention. Pure bliss.

Can't say I blame her.

The man possesses the most talented digits on the planet.

Brain, please stick to neutral and PG-rated topics.

Too late, as the memory of our night together once again invades my every cell—his long fingers wrapped around my hips as he sank inside me, his gaze never wavering from my face as he whispered how spectacular I felt. How beautiful I was at that moment.

Damn, but he's good.

"At least you and Ash aren't at war anymore." Mina's statement interrupts my thoughts, and I shoot her a smile before reaching over to squeeze her arm.

"I didn't realize it was so hard on you guys. I'm sorry about that."

Mina waves her hand, dismissing my apology. "Don't worry about it. Besides, it's all in the past. You two kissed and made up, just like I said you should."

Mina is lucky I love her. Otherwise, I'd push her pretty ass into the nearest snowbank for her continuous intimations.

"Are you going to drop it?"

"Never. Way too much fun to mess with you." She jerks her chin in Ash's direction. "Why don't you go over and talk to him?"

"And say what? Excuse me, may I cut through your throng of fans? Let me take a number for a moment of your time? Hard pass." I shake my head and focus my attention on a velvet drape, running my hand along the soft fabric. "I'm happy here on the fringes."

"Maybe he's waiting for you to talk to him."

A snort of laughter flies out of my mouth as I point toward Ash and his eager fan club. "Does he look like he's waiting? Trust me, the last thing I need is a man with that much competition."

"With the right man, there wouldn't be any competition."

Mina's sentiment vaguely echoes what Ash told me during our night together. How the *right* man would claim me, not wait for me to do the heavy lifting.

Case in point: Asher Hammond is *not* that man, no matter what my hormones say.

I wave my hands around, grateful my friend and I are on the same page. "Exactly. I need one of those. Know where I might find one around here?"

"One what?" a deep voice inquires behind me—a voice with which I'm very familiar.

Crap. How much did he hear?

A slow smile stretches Mina's face as she gazes over my shoulder. "Ori needs a good man. Know of anyone who might be interested?"

My face flames hot at my coworker's words.

Seriously, woman, please shut up.

"Oh look, cookies. Have to grab one of those." Mina scampers across the tent, but I catch the triumphant smirk on her face as she passes.

I'm definitely firing her later.

"I have a present for you," Ash says.

Turning on my heel, I accept the cup of steaming liquid

that he offers with a smile. "Mulled wine. So, this is where that delicious smell was coming from. Thank you."

He shoves his hands in his jeans and scuffs his boot across the pavement. "I figured you might be cold. Seems all the other women out here are freezing their asses off."

"Might have something to do with their attire, or lack thereof."

"Tell me something." He jerks his thumb toward a small group of women huddled around the heater. "Why do women dress like that and then complain they're cold?"

He can't be serious with this question.

Rolling my eyes, I take a sip of my wine. "You know *exactly* why they're dressed like that."

"I do?"

"Don't play dumb. They, like every other woman out here, want a chance with you."

"Interesting theory."

"It's not a theory."

Ash's gaze roves the length of me, a smirk coloring his mouth. "If that's the case, then how come you're *not* dressed like that?"

Conceited prick.

No way will I give his ego that level of satisfaction, especially not after he shot me down for a second round.

He can butter up his harem if he requires accolades.

"It's simple. At my age, I'm far too practical to catch pneumonia, hoping to catch a man's eye." I pull my glasses down and peer at him over my lenses. "Plus, I'm not looking for a spot in your rotation."

Aloof and haughty bitch, at your service.

My barb hits its target as the smile falls from Ash's face.

He crosses his arms over his broad chest, rocking back on his heels. "Good to know."

Damn it.

Now, I feel guilty about my snarky comment, which is ridiculous. First, Ash knows he's adored. He's got a line of women—a literal line—ready to service his every need.

Second, it's not like the man actually cares how I view him. I'm one voice in a sea of hundreds.

Third, and the *biggest* reason, I asked him out. He shot me down. If anything, I should be the one who's pissed.

Come to think of it, I guess I am.

Still, I hate being that person. Jealousy is a terrible look and even though I wounded his ego, he hasn't stalked off, despite my caustic retort.

Time to ease the tension in this conversation. I lean into him, giving him a teasing nudge. "There must be one holdout in your crowd of adoring fans. Otherwise, it's too easy and where is the fun in that?"

Ash glances down at where I nudged him, his expression softening just a touch. The pressure eases, but there's still a flicker of unresolved emotion in his eyes.

"Maybe you're right," he says, as his gaze wanders over the throng of women awaiting his affections. "Too easy gets boring after a while."

"I'll give you this, Mr. Hammond. You're never boring."

"Neither are you, Ms. Thorne."

"That's Ms. Frost Queen to you," I retort, the sassy edge lining my words, as I bite back a smile.

Ash catches me off guard when he wraps an arm around my shoulder, pulling me toward him. I glance up at him, momentarily frozen by the intensity of his stare. "No matter how it looks, don't read too much into it."

What the hell does that mean? Don't read into our one-night stand and his subsequent blow-off? Don't read into the cluster of women desperate to spend an hour alone with him? Don't read into this moment?

Nice try, Ash, but I'm reading into *all* of it.

I need distance. Preferably a safe distance of fifty miles or so, but since that isn't an option, I'll go with my second-best bet.

Stepping from his side, I allow us both some breathing room. I motion to the table and chairs at the far end of the tent. "Your tent is popular. Is it strictly because you're playing Santa later or am I missing something?"

Ash quirks his brow at me. "I'm playing Santa?"

"Of sorts. To one or more of these women, anyway. Fulfilling their Christmas wish list."

He snorts out a laugh and shakes his head before tugging a hand through his hair. "We've got the bar and photo booth, which is always a hit, plus I'm doing a live demonstration later. We're raffling off a custom piece."

"You can create a custom piece that quickly?" I release a low whistle. "Impressive."

"It's actually a list of people who tossed their names in a jar over the last month. They're already signed up to get the work done, but there's a waiting list. Six months, at this point. The winner jumps the line and gets their approved design inked today. Although I'd like to claim that I can sketch up a custom piece in twenty minutes, I'm not *that* good."

"Oh yes, you are," I volley back. "And you know you are."

A smile creases his face, those dimples evident beneath his beard. "I meant tattooing."

I press my hand to my chest as I plaster on my best shocked expression. "Obviously. What did you think I meant?"

He leans in, his breath at my ear. "Don't you dare play innocent. I know how wild you are. You and that smart mouth of yours."

No, no, no. He is not allowed to segue into sexually charged comments anymore.

But since he is, I'm standing my ground. "Didn't hear you complaining that night."

"Why would I? You were fabulous. But be warned. You keep sassing me, and I'll have to put that mouth of yours to better use."

How typical. "I'm sure you have plenty of women to fill that position."

"That I want to hear screaming my name as I devour every inch of her?" He skews his mouth to the right, his eyes sparking fire at me. "Not at all."

I have two options: continue down this heated path about sensual exploits or ignore his comment and move on to casual conversation.

This time, I'm playing it safe.

My heart and ego still carry bruises from the last time.

Time to turn the focus to his upcoming sexual Olympics, with at least twelve women in contention for a medal.

Taking another sip of wine, I step out from under his arm and twirl around, noting the stern glares coming from the contenders. Seems they don't like me wasting their man's precious time.

Tough shit, ladies. I'm hardly holding him against his will.

Maybe they fail to realize that playing too easily into Ash's hand might render the opposite effect. Perhaps he wants to chat with someone who isn't undressing him with their eyes and hanging on his every word.

Either way, he's still here with me.

For whatever reason.

"I see you scoping out the place. What are you searching for—an escape route?" Ash asks, giving me a cocky grin. "There isn't one, you know. You're stuck."

"Damn it. Thought I might make a quick getaway."

"Running away from me again?"

I shrug, allowing another swallow of the spiced wine to slide down my throat. "Maybe. Sue me, okay? I'm surrounded by Asher Hammond's hall of fame, which is not a place I ever wanted to visit. You have more trophies than the Yankees."

Ash rubs a hand over his brow, but he doesn't deny my claim. Why bother? We both know the truth. "Contrary to what you think, I haven't slept with *any* of these women."

"Not yet, but that will change before the end of the night." And that knowledge makes me sick to my stomach.

"Do I get a say in these activities, or is it preordained?"

I arch my brow at him and release a heated sigh. "Like you'd say no."

"Jesus, what you must think of me?" A muscle ticks in Ash's jaw as he huffs out a breath. But again, he's hardly denying my words. "What about you? How many men do you plan to take home tonight?"

I sputter my wine, wiping the stray drop from my lips. "How about none?" I gesture down the length of my body before meeting his stare. "I reserve these curves for a select few."

What I don't mention? That he's the first man I've slept with in nine months. My guess is he's slept with ten times that many women in the last week.

There's that damn nausea again.

But although my statement could be construed as a compliment, it's obvious Ash isn't taking it that way.

He averts his eyes, focusing on the far side of the tent. "How many men are in this select group?"

Odd question.

I tilt my head to peer up at him, my lips curled into a teasing smile. "Why do you want to know?"

Ash shrugs and cracks his knuckles as a ripple of tension shoots through him. "Have to know how many asses I need to kick."

A thrill rips through me at his reply, even if it's likely just bravado. "Hmm. Interesting."

"Are you going to answer my question?"

I shake my head and take another swallow of wine, even though I can't hide the smile crossing my face. "Nope."

"Really, and why not?"

"Way more fun this way," I reply with a wink and a quick hip check. "Besides, I don't care to know *your* number. No way can I fight off that many women."

Ash chuckles, the deep sound vibrating through his chest. "You'd fight these women over me?"

"Only to defend your honor." I set my wine down and raise my fists, adopting a boxer's stance. "As you can see, I'm fierce and highly intimidating."

A full belly laugh breaks from Ash's throat as he looks

down at me, his eyes crinkling with mischief. "Not the adjectives I'd choose for you, but I appreciate the sentiment, Little One."

Little One. It's hardly the first time someone has commented on my size, but it's the way he speaks the words. There's a warm affection lining each syllable.

Or maybe the mulled wine is getting to me and I'm seeing things that aren't there.

Again.

I lower my fists and relax my posture. "What adjectives *would* you choose to describe me?"

Ash wraps his arm around my waist, hauling me close again. "No way. You have to answer first. How many asses am I kicking?"

He says the words against my ear, his mouth lingering against my skin a second longer than necessary, and I fight to maintain our cordial camaraderie as my heart hammers in my chest.

I swallow, my mouth suddenly dry. "Not nearly as many as I am. Let's leave it at that. Now, it's time to turn the focus onto *you*. See that woman? The one with the short blonde hair?"

Ash follows my gaze to the woman leaning against the bar, but he doesn't release his grip on my waist. "What about her?"

"She told me personally that she dressed like that for you."

Ash snorts out a laugh. "She hasn't said a word to me."

"Said plenty to me."

"Wait a damn minute. Why were you talking about me? Are you two friends?"

"Contrary to popular belief, not all of my conversations

revolve around you." I lean to the side and snatch my glass of wine off the table, acutely aware that Ash's arms remain wrapped around me.

Trust me, I'm not the only one who's noticed. There will no doubt be a contract on my life for Ash's public display of affection toward me.

Eh, his embrace might be worth dying for.

"I've never seen her before today. She asked to use my bathroom, right before intimating she planned to feast on *you* for supper."

Ash shoots me a grin, an amused sparkle in his eyes. "That's quite the claim. You let her get away with that?"

"What was I supposed to do? Beat her up?"

"Hey, you're the one who offered to defend my honor."

"So, you're not interested in her services?" Of course, my question is dual-sided. This man is a conundrum.

He considers my question, no doubt aware of the scowl crossing my features with every passing second. "It's an interesting offer," he mumbles, biting back yet another smile.

Oh, he wants to play it that way. Fine by me.

"One might say it is. Want me to introduce you? Get the show started?" I pull away from Ash and turn in the woman's direction. Time for a little fun with our resident Romeo.

"Hell no." Ash grabs me back, pulling me flush against him, my back pressed to his chest. "You are staying right here."

Another surge of heat courses through me, chasing away any lingering chill. But I refuse to let Ash in on that fact.

"Are you using me as a human shield now?" I tease,

aware of the daggers being shot my way by the surrounding women.

Looks like *I* need the damn shield more than he does.

"I think I'd aim for someone slightly bigger for that task."

"I'm not *that* little," I mutter, my bottom lip protruding in a pout.

"Yes, you are, but you're also tough as nails. Scared the hell out of me for six months. That's why you're my new bodyguard."

I laugh and take another drink of wine. "Nice try, but I don't think you can afford my services. I don't come cheap."

"I'm fighting off an army of men and you won't even offer your bodyguard skills against one woman? What happened to my tough little warrior?"

"What a load of crap. You're not fighting anyone over me." There is a bluntness to my words. I'm not challenging him to disagree. Why would I when I already know his response?

Ash pushes my hair over my shoulder, his fingers gliding across my neck and setting every nerve cell abuzz. "Watch me. That select few you mentioned will be zero before the day is out, because I don't share."

Chapter 12

The Cost of Temptation

Ori

How the hell am I *not* supposed to read into that statement? The man is a walking contradiction. He doesn't want me, but he'll be damned if anyone else has me.

Make it make sense.

I need space. When I'm this close to Ash, my head gets fuzzy and don't even get me started on the feelings coursing through the rest of my body.

But when I try to pull away, his grip only tightens, his fingers unyielding as his lips once again dip to my ear. "Where are you running off to, Little One? I'm nowhere near ready to let you go."

He opens a button on my coat and slips his hand beneath the woolen fabric. My breath hitches as his fingers dip under my sweater to trace slow, deliberate lines across my stomach, sending a wave of warmth that curls low in my core.

I bite back a gasp as my body arches involuntarily into

his touch, craving more even as I struggle to resist his advances. "Ash—"

"I need this. I need you." His mouth grazes the sensitive skin beneath my ear, his beard delivering a delicious tickle that shoots another surge of sparks through me. "Back to your bodyguard services. Think I can make alternate payment arrangements?"

"I'm open to negotiations." My words are a husky whisper, evidence of his effect on me.

"Lucky for me, I possess insider information."

"On what?"

"On you." He brushes his nose along my jaw before nipping at my earlobe, the sensation sending a jolt of electricity through me.

I duck my head, desperate to keep my wits about me. "That tickles."

"That's the idea." Another chuckle rumbles from his chest, reverberating through me. Ash is savoring every second of undoing me.

Seems he doesn't mind an audience. Come to think of it, neither do I, at least not where Asher Hammond is concerned, and I'm sure as hell not telling him to stop. At this point, every word is a struggle against the illicit battle he's waging.

Although his movements hide beneath the fabric of my coat, one look at my face will tell people all they need to know about our current activity. Thank God for the dim lighting and dark velvet drapes.

Ash continues his covert exploration as he slides his hand beneath the waist of my pants, tracing along the edge of my g-string. Then he dips lower, dancing his fingers across my clit as his talented digits beckon me out to play. "Fuck, Oriana Thorne, the feel of you. You are pure temptation."

Will I have sex here in the far corner of the tent? At this moment, it's a definite option. I'll deal with any public relations nightmare another day.

Right now, my body is driven by nothing but desire.

"Want to go inside?" Ash murmurs, his voice a low growl in my ear.

Before I can respond in the affirmative and drag him to our basement hideaway, someone clears their throat next to us, cutting off our stolen moment.

Glancing to my left, I spy Braden, a knowing smile quirking the corners of his mouth. "Sorry to interrupt, but I need to steal my brother."

I expect Ash to release me immediately, now that his brother—and the rest of the patrons in the tent—are fully aware of our ministrations.

But I'm wrong. Ash cocks a brow at Braden, but his hand remains splayed against my abdomen. "I'm a little busy. What do you need?"

Braden shakes his head with a laugh. "I can see that, but we're about to pick the raffle winner, and since you're the artist laying the ink, that job falls to you."

Then he turns and walks away, no doubt enjoying a silent snicker for catching us with our pants almost down—again.

Ash drops his head to my shoulder with a grunt. "Perfect timing, as always."

"Duty calls."

He slips his hand from beneath my coat, and my skin

immediately misses the warmth of his caress. "I'll catch up with you later, okay?"

I spin around and offer a cheeky smile as I catch Ash adjusting himself. Glad to know I have some effect on the man. "Don't go too far. A bodyguard is always on duty."

He glances down at me, a small smile tugging at his lips. "Thought you said I couldn't afford you?"

I trace the rim of my wine glass and shrug. "Eh, we'll work out a payment schedule. I'm certain you can come up with something to satisfy my demands."

"Satisfying your demands might become my full-time job," he says, his voice a low rumble as he slides a finger along my jaw.

"Worse ways to go."

Ash chortles, running a hand along the back of his neck. "Damn straight."

Do I want to delay the end of our flirtation? Of course, but I see Braden out of the corner of my eye, jerking his chin toward the waiting crowd at the far end of the tent.

I give Ash a playful shove. "Go on. I'm heading down the street to grab some food."

Ash gestures behind him. "The guys are ordering pizza. You're welcome to a slice."

There's something about his current demeanor that is so endearing. Even if he plays the part of the big, tough heartbreaker, I can tell he's reluctant to leave my side.

Maybe it's because he was guaranteed a quick fuck in the basement. Or maybe, just maybe, he likes me, too. Even if he won't admit that fact.

"I heard there is a champagne and chocolate set up outside the wine bar, and I'm dying to taste some chocolate right now."

Ash averts his gaze, barking out a laugh. "Dying, huh?"

"Absolutely desperate. My mouth is watering already." I drag my tongue along my lower lip and release a low moan.

"Fucking hell," Ash mutters, grabbing at his jeans to adjust himself once more. "You don't play fair."

Biting my lip, I hold his gaze. He may have to leave, but I'm ensuring I remain at the forefront of his thoughts. "Where's the fun in that? Now scoot. Go pick your lucky winner."

My gaze follows Ash as he saunters across the tent, ready to choose the lucky recipient of his custom-made body art. If the gods are kind, it'll be a burly man who wins the prize.

Turns out, the gods are sadistic assholes. I grit my teeth as Ash selects the winner from the glass bowl—a striking woman with inky black hair, a wisp of a waist and the biggest tits I've seen outside of the porn industry.

Mina sidles over, a mischievous gleam in her eye. "Having fun?"

"Not at the moment," I grumble, shooting a side-eye toward Ash and the dark-haired beauty captivating his attention.

"Not now. Before."

"It was fine," I lie, determined to downplay my stolen moments with Sparkwood's resident heartthrob. "Why?"

Mina shakes her head, releasing an aggravated grunt. "Fine? What a load of garbage. I saw you two canoodling."

Despite my internal angst, I chuckle and down my last sip of wine. "That is a bald-faced lie. I never canoodle. For your information, I'm Ash's new bodyguard."

"Is that what you two are calling it?"

"What would *you* call it?"

"Totally fucking hot for one another." She wags her finger under my nose. "Don't deny it. Everyone in this tent saw what happened between you two."

"Great, I'll likely have a hit out on me by the end of the festival." I brush imaginary lint from my coat, trying my damnedest to put my emotions back to rights. "Maybe he did it to get a rise out of them. Stoke their jealousy. Stranger things have happened."

Mina rolls her eyes. "Or maybe Ash did it to send a message."

"What message is that?"

"Back off, because he's off the market."

Now I've heard everything. Yes, the romantic idealist in me yearns for that to be the case, but the realistic side of my nature warns me it's highly unlikely. Does Ash like me? Probably. Thinks I'm great in the sack? I'm leaning toward yes. Willing to part with his player persona for me? Let's not get ahead of ourselves.

"Trust me, not even close. I've been hired for my extraordinary sparring skills. End of story."

I hug myself as the brisk chill sweeps in from the tent entrance. Funny how I didn't feel the cold in Ash's arms. But it's back to reality.

At least for the present.

"Obviously. What other reason could he have?" Mina motions toward the store. "Ready to head out for a bit? Check out the rest of the festival?"

"Absolutely. Want to join me for some champagne and chocolate at the wine bar?"

Mina's eyes light up like a kid at, well, Christmas. "Definitely."

I cast one final glance toward Ash before ducking out of

the tent, but he's too involved with Ms. Porn USA to notice me.

Yet another reason keeping my distance is the smart move. There is no way I can share a man with a bevy of other women—that's just not in my DNA.

But with Asher Hammond, that's my only option.

Chapter 13

A League of Her Own

Ori

So much for champagne and chocolate.

What was supposed to be a quick dash into the store to check on the staff swiftly turned into an all hands on deck situation.

Seems we aren't the only ones craving a bit of warmth. One More Page is hopping, with a steady line for both the register and the coffee bar. Plus, another dozen customers mill about the store's interior, engaging in the age old pastime of browsing.

Is there anything better than scanning the shelves of books before settling into a leather-backed chair by the pot-bellied stove?

I mean, besides play time with Asher Hammond. Despite the hustle and bustle, my mind continues to wander to Mr. Tall, Dark & Infuriatingly Handsome. If Braden hadn't interrupted us in the tent, would Ash have made good on his offer?

Better question is, would I have taken him up on said offer with a string of townsfolk within earshot?

We all know the answer to that question. I have the backbone of a marshmallow where that man is concerned.

After ninety minutes, the hubbub settles down, and my stomach growls with an urgent plea. I need food and chocolate will not cut it at this point.

Maybe I should grab a slice of pizza. Hey, Ash offered me some earlier.

Besides, that keeps me close to the store in case anyone needs me.

It's not like I'm desperate to see him or anything. Not at all.

But to get said pizza, I will have to wander back into Black Lotus's tent.

Plus, I am moonlighting as Ash's bodyguard, so regular check-ins are imperative to ensure the man's well-being.

Nothing else to see here, folks.

As luck would have it, Ash is nowhere to be found, and neither is that now cold pizza. So, to avoid looking like I'm tracking him down, I whisper a silent plea to my stomach for a few minutes of cooperation and focus my attention on the tattoo portfolios sitting atop a long table.

I'll give it to the men of Black Lotus. They are seriously talented artists. Each one possesses their own style, but the quality throughout is impeccable. My fingers drift over pictures of Ash's work—large scale photorealistic portraits and landscapes with as much intricate detail as a photograph. Even when I lean close, examining the artwork, I fail to find one line or dot out of place.

They're perfect, much like the man himself. Perfectly unattainable, at least.

"Looking for some ink?"

I cut my gaze to Braden, who's lounging in a chair at the far end of the table. "Just browsing."

He waves me over, patting a chair next to him. "Come on, sit down."

"Oh, I—"

A smile cuts across Braden's features as he holds up a paintbrush, pointing to a sign above the table offering custom body painting. "Don't worry. It's temporary."

"No way. It's far too cold to strip down for body painting." I hug myself tight, earning a guffaw from Braden.

"How about your arm? Think you could bear baring it for me?"

His upbeat attitude is infectious, and I relent to his request, sinking into the empty chair. Pulling off my glove and shoving up my sleeve, I offer my arm up as Braden's canvas.

Braden sets to work, opening a few paint colors before grasping my wrist to draw an outline of a lily on my forearm. He focuses on his craft, which allows me a few minutes to focus on him.

Like Ash, he's also covered in colorful ink, with longish dark hair that always seems a bit tousled, and green eyes that are just a shade darker than his brother's. A gorgeous specimen, to be sure, but without the cocky charisma that pulses through every cell of Asher Hammond. No, Braden is quieter, more subdued, and though admiring glances are often thrown his way, he's not the kind of man who thrives on flirtation.

Too bad I have a ridiculous crush on the playboy half of the Hammond brothers, because Braden is undoubtedly the safer bet for my heart. But hearts don't give a damn about safety nets or security. They leap headfirst into the abyss without bothering to check if there's water in the pool.

That, and Braden belongs to Mina. Even if he doesn't know it yet.

"Damn. You're drawing that freehand? You're good."

Braden chuckles, his gaze focused downward. "I've always loved painting, but I'm nowhere near as talented as Ash."

"That's not true."

Braden shrugs and dips his brush into a deep red. "Sadly, it is. His portraiture and realism skills are ridiculous. Did you check out his portfolio?"

"I did, along with yours. Don't sell yourself short. That fox tattoo you created is stunning."

He bites his lip, a soft smile on his mouth. "Thanks. One of my favorites, too. Ash has always pushed the envelope with ink. I stick to neo-traditional tattoos—animals, birds, flowers."

"Good thing I like animals, birds and flowers." I'm not sure why, but I feel the need to bolster Braden's ego. Although I know he and Ash are close, I get the distinct impression he lives in Ash's shadow.

How can he not? Ash is larger than life, both in reputation and ego. Just ask his fan club, which accepts countless new members daily.

Still, it's obvious Braden is proud of his big brother and I know the feeling is mutual. I wish I had a sibling. It's difficult growing up as an only child—there's this invisible drive to be all things to all people and that is a recipe for disaster.

"Hey, I wanted to thank you. Ash told me you signed the revised lease."

"Happy to help. Really happy we're not at war anymore."

Braden nods and rolls his eyes, giving me a good-natured chuckle. "We're all thankful for that."

"Sorry. I didn't realize the toll it took on everyone."

Braden switches colors, highlighting the petals with a delicate pink. "Let's put it this way. You two are far more fun to be around now."

"When we're not trying to kill each other, you mean?" I sniffle and rub my nose with my free hand, acutely aware of the falling temperature inside the tent. "You think we'll get snow tonight? It smells like it."

"Let's hope not, because Ash rode in on his bike today. I've traveled on two wheels during a snowstorm, and I don't recommend it."

"Maybe you could give him a lift home, should he require it?"

He shoots me a sly look from under the brim of his baseball cap. "Maybe you could, since you two are friends now."

Are we though? We've fucked. An epic fuck, to be sure, but it was a one-night stand. If my store wasn't next door to Ash's parlor, would I have ever seen him again? Better question, if I didn't hold half the rights to the basement, would that one night together have happened in the first place?

I'm not one to ruminate on my decisions. A good time is a good time, and I'm far past the age of berating myself for caving to carnal pleasures. But what happens when you want more than one night?

"Ash has dreamed of opening a speakeasy in Sparkwood for years, and it's the perfect spot for it,"

Braden continues. "Trust me, he'll make sure it doesn't hurt your store in any way. He'll take care of you."

Good to know, although Braden's definition of care no doubt differs from my own.

"What the fuck are you doing?"

Braden and I snap our heads up in unison as Ash's voice slices through our conversation, sharp and heated.

"She's trying some ink on for size," Braden replies with a shrug as he returns his attention to my skin, adding a few finishing touches to the leaves. "Ori has such pale skin, so the color pops."

But instead of admiring the delicate flower decorating my forearm, Ash continues to glare holes into his brother.

Braden sets the brush to the side and shakes his head with a chuckle. He doesn't bother to hide his amusement over Ash's obvious annoyance.

Not that I'm entirely sure *why* Ash is so damn aggravated.

"That'll do it," Braden proclaims. "The ink stays on the skin for several days, but the more you wash the area, the faster it fades. I'm off to grab a drink. See you later, Ori."

I trace a finger along my arm, careful not to smudge the still tacky ink. "Thanks for the lily."

Ash sinks into his brother's vacated chair and reaches for my arm, a grimace creasing his features. "At least it's temporary."

What an odd sentiment from a tattoo artist, especially when the design in question is high quality.

"Braden is very talented and I've considered getting a tattoo. This seems like a good spot for one and a flower is so delicate and feminine—"

"No."

My eyes search out Ash's, shocked by his forceful reply. "Excuse me?"

Ash shrugs, as if his demand is the most normal response in the world. "Some women are born to wear ink. Others aren't."

I stiffen at his insinuation, jerking my gaze to the floor as a surge of anger shoots through me. "And I'm the latter, I suppose."

"Exactly." He slides a finger beneath my chin, tipping my head up. "You're perfect, just as you are. You don't need any of this."

What Asher Hammond doesn't realize is he just gave me the greatest compliment of my life. I've always opted to blend into the background, seeking safety in the shadows. That a man like Ash, with throngs of women clamoring for his attention, considers me the ideal, is mind-boggling.

It's also turned on a very different emotion—one that involves a dimly lit basement and our favorite couch.

A flush climbs my cheeks as his fingers make meandering circles along my inner wrist. "Can't say that's a very good business plan for the owner of a tattoo parlor."

Ash grins, his sex on a stick dimple at the ready. "Maybe that's because I want a different kind of business with you."

Yes, please. In every language.

Okay, under normal circumstances, I would never ask a man out again when he's already shot me down once, but this isn't a normal situation.

There's no way Ash doesn't feel something for me, even if most of that feeling is below the waist.

Not after spouting that indescribably romantic line.

Ash grabs a gauze pad and piece of plastic film, placing

it over my newly acquired skin art. "Don't want it to smudge."

"Yes, you do. You want it gone," I tease.

He offers another shrug as he pulls my sleeve down to cover my arm. "Braden is right. The ink really pops on your fair skin."

"Does that mean you've adopted a new stance on me and tattoos?"

"Not at all."

I lean my arms on the table and suck in a deep breath, fully prepared to make a fool of myself again. "Think I can steal you away for a minute?"

Ash matches my posture, our faces mere inches apart. "What do you have in mind?"

"Food."

"Damn, I thought you had a different idea entirely." He leans back against his chair and strokes a hand along his jaw. "I just got back from that wine bar you mentioned, but I'll go again."

A furrow creases my brow. "You already went?"

Maybe he went looking for me, since I'd mentioned I would be there.

Ash nods, averting his gaze. "Yeah. Raven was hungry, so I took her to grab a bite. No alcohol, for obvious reasons, but they had all sorts of food. Brilliant suggestion."

Or maybe I never even crossed his mind. Instead, he used my recommendation as a pseudo date with another woman.

Just like that, his earlier compliment fades into the ether, leaving nothing but a gnawing jealousy in the pit of my stomach.

I don't bother asking which woman out of the many

meandering about the area is Raven. What's the point? Bruise my ego a bit more this afternoon?

I clear my throat and slide on my gloves. "Glad to hear it was good, although I'm past the point of chocolate curing what ails me. I need something more substantial."

Ash motions over his shoulder toward Black Lotus. "There's plenty of pizza left."

Which sounds as appetizing as being Ash's second run to the wine bar. "Hmm. Cold pizza or hot soup. Tough decision."

He laughs and shakes his head. "Mental note: woman hates pizza."

I wag a finger at him before standing. "No, no, no. I adore pizza and I eat it all the time, but I'm craving something different. Know what I mean?"

I also need to get the hell out of here and put some space between me and Sparkwood's resident playboy.

The smile drops from Ash's face, replaced by a hunger as his gaze roams over me. "I absolutely do."

Sadly, that comment has zero effect on me, considering he likely said something similar to Raven or Dove or whatever other bird he's courting—and escorting—into bed today.

Lucky for me, someone else is looking for Asher Hammond. Miracle of miracles, it's also not a woman.

Zane pokes his head into the tent, rolling his eyes when he spots Ash. "There you are. I've been looking everywhere for you. Your custom is waiting inside."

"Already?" Ash pulls out his phone, a scoff escaping his lips when he spies the time. "Guess time really does fly when you're having fun."

"Your custom?" I ask, burrowing my face into the warmth of my scarf.

"Custom ink piece. The winner from earlier today."

Ah yes, who can forget the gothic playboy bunny with legs for days and tits the size of cantaloupes?

Sadly, I do not possess a poker face. Every emotion shows and this time, I feel the aggravation slide across my features.

Ash notices it, too.

A low chuckle rises from his chest as he stretches, his gaze fixed on me. "You can keep hiding in that scarf, but I know what you're thinking."

"That I'm freezing?"

He leans in, his mouth a gentle whisper at my ear. "That you're jealous."

What an arrogant know-it-all.

"Not possible. I already told you, Ash, I'm not looking to be a part of your rotation."

But instead of the thin-lipped reply from earlier, his face settles into a full grin as he playfully leans in to press a kiss to my cheek. "You're in a league of your own, Oriana Thorne. No one even comes close."

I hate how smooth he is with these lines. How very honest they feel as they dance across my heartstrings.

I motion toward the tent entrance. "You better go. Don't want to keep your custom waiting."

Ash nods and stands, but pauses, focusing his gaze on me. "Since I don't have time right now, how about you set aside some time tonight? After I finish up, I'll take you to the wine bar or wherever you want to go. Sound good?"

It sounds amazing, but I refuse to cave *that* easily.

Yes, of course I'm going to cave, but I have to put up a mild show of resistance—even if he sees right through it.

"Setting aside time for little old me? Well, aren't I special?" I reply, shooting him a coy wink from behind my glasses.

"You most definitely are."

"Maybe after I grab some food, I'll head over to Black Lotus and watch you work. I'd like to see you in action." I bite my lip, fully aware of the double entendre of my statement.

Ash also latches onto my words. He steps closer and wraps his hands around my waist, pulling me flush against him. "Thought you already had. Looking for some new ideas?"

Gliding my tongue along my lower lip, I gaze up at him through lowered lashes, desperately trying to appear unaffected by his proximity. "Told you I'm hungry. In truth, I possess an insatiable appetite."

"Fucking hell, woman." Ash mutters the words, but his dimpled smile assures me it's meant in the best fashion. "You're really fucking pretty, you know that?"

Warmth floods my cells again as his green eyes study me, threatening to short circuit my brain's attempt to hold the man at arm's length.

"I could say the same about you."

A guffaw slips past his mouth. "I am *not* pretty. Take that back."

"Fine. Hot as hell. Better?"

"Getting there. We'll work on it later."

Zane clears his throat, ending our playful banter. Seems his chronically late employee is suddenly running a tight ship. "Come on, man. She's waiting."

With a final chuckle and roll of his eyes, Ash releases his grip on me and strolls over to Zane, giving his employee a playful punch in the shoulder. "Why are you in such a damn hurry all of a sudden?"

"Because," Zane replies, flexing his tattooed arms as he drums the air, "the sooner you're finished, the sooner we get down to the business of some serious fun. A few of the chicks have decided to stay the night in Sparkwood. Rented a suite at the hotel. The rest, as they say, shall go down in history."

From my vantage point, I can't hear Ash's response to Zane as they walk inside Black Lotus, although I'm hopeful he'll forgo the party for some up close and personal fun with me.

After all, he was the one who brought up spending time together, and if the look in his eyes was anything to hang my hat on, he's all too eager for a second night of fun.

No, I'm not reading into it. I'm fully aware of Ash's position on dating.

But isn't every man footloose and fancy free until they meet the right woman?

Why can't I be that woman? Ash already mentioned how different I am from his usual hookups—isn't that a good thing?

In a league of my own.

Yes, it's *definitely* a good thing.

I walk out of the tent and raise my hand to catch Mina's attention across the parking lot.

She hurries over, rubbing her hands together briskly. "Damn, but it's cold. Did you get any food yet? Braden mentioned they have—"

"Don't say the word pizza," I warn her with a chuckle.

"Fine. How about soup and a sandwich from the deli?"

"Perfect." I link arms with Mina as we stroll down the brightly lit sidewalk, dodging a vibrant mix of festival goers along the way.

"How is Ash?" Mina asks, a small smile playing on her mouth.

"Fine. He's doing a live demonstration soon. I thought we could head over there after we eat." I skew my mouth to the side and avert my gaze. "You could hang out with Braden some more."

Mina laughs as a flush climbs her cheeks. "Sure, that's why you want to hang out there. So I can talk to Braden."

"Obviously. What other reason might I have?"

My friend pulls open the deli door, holding it for me. "You're the worst liar. Just admit you've got a thing for Asher Hammond."

"Never."

"Still a liar," she responds in a sing-song voice before turning her attention to the case of pre-made sandwiches.

I catch my reflection in the mirror hanging over the deli counter—the long dark hair, cheeks pinked from the cold, full lips and dark eyes dancing behind my lenses—and recall Ash's compliment as he held me in his arms.

Really fucking pretty.

There was something so genuine and endearing about his words, as if he never imagined this thing happening between us, but now that it has, he's okay with the idea.

I shake my head, trying to clear the thoughts. *It's just a passing flirtation. Right?*

Mina turns back with a grin. "You're blushing. Don't even try to deny it this time."

"Maybe it's a two-way street." That's as much as I'll offer, but for my friend, it's enough.

She wraps an arm about my shoulder, giving me a quick hug. "I don't think there's any maybe about it."

A smile splits my face as I give the deli worker my order, but Mina's words dance along the edges of my mind.

She's right. I need to stop overthinking this situation with Ash and just let it unfold. It's obvious he likes me and tonight, we'll see how much.

But for now, I'm content with the fact that in a room of half-naked women, all desperate for the man's attention, I was the only one he saw.

Chapter 14

Caught Red-Handed

Ori

After a quick bite to eat, Mina and I hightail it back to the store. We duck inside to let the staff know we'll return in an hour to relieve them before walking next door to Black Lotus.

I've only been inside one other time, and let's be honest, I was too damn angry to appreciate the upscale decor.

My knowledge of tattoo parlors is nil, but Black Lotus reeks of sophistication and understated elegance.

Sleek pieces of artwork line the walls, no doubt courtesy of the resident artists, and soft lighting casts a gentle glow over the reception area. Two leather loungers and a dark green velvet couch sit against the far wall, currently occupied by a handful of tattooed beauties, their inked skin an extension of the artistry displayed on the walls. The space feels inviting, yet there's an undeniable edge to it, a blend of luxury and creativity that's both alluring and slightly intimidating.

His world is so different from mine. I don't belong here, do I?

I only allow the thought to linger for a moment before

kicking it aside. When given free rein, my brain never fails to drag me to the darkest emotional crevices, threatening to pitch my happiness over the edge without so much as a backward glance. But not today. Today, I refuse to let doubt take root.

"I'm impressed," I murmur to Mina. "It's more gallery than grunge."

"Almost like they're not the heathens you believed them to be," Mina replies with a snort.

"Remind me again why we're friends."

"Because you love me and can't live without me."

Now it's my turn to snort out a laugh. "Keep telling yourself that."

Granted, every word is true. I'd be lost without Mina. She's the little sister I never had.

We weave through the crowd of twenty or so people until we have a clear view of Ash and his workspace. It's not as close as I'd prefer, but I have the distinct feeling if I push these folks out of the way, they'll return the favor.

Ash perches on a low stool, his gloved hands arranging the inks in front of him. He moves with the practiced ease of a man who knows exactly what he's doing and how fabulous he is at doing it. Every motion is confident, calculated. Once again, not a hint of insecurity, just the quiet swagger of a man who's a master of his craft.

A master with women, too.

Ash glances at his client, shooting her a lopsided grin. "While I finish getting ready, why don't you introduce yourself, gorgeous?"

Their gazes lock for a beat before she offers a wave and sexy smile to the crowd.

I thought she was striking from a distance, but I was

mistaken. Striking is an understatement. The woman is stunning—a sexually charged mash-up of Snow White and Jessica Rabbit—with long jet-black hair and skin just a shade darker than mine. But unlike me, several pieces of ink highlight her skin.

Tugging up the sleeve of my sweater, I glance at the now dry lily painted on my forearm and wonder why she suits the inked look, and I don't.

Hating how her beauty blends effortlessly with Ash's chiseled good looks, while I'm a puzzle piece that doesn't quite fit, no matter how you position it.

Maybe this was a bad idea.

"What's your name, beautiful?" a man calls out from the crowd.

The dark-haired woman smiles in his direction. "Hi, lover. My name is Raven Scarlett, but you can call me baby."

"Oh, baby," the man in the crowd responds, letting loose with a wolf whistle.

Of course, Raven's voice is soft and breathy, a la Marilyn Monroe. A bedroom voice to match her bedroom eyes and bedroom curves.

She's a walking, talking wet dream, and the crowd is eating her up.

Mina jostles me in the ribs. "Raven Scarlett? What kind of name is that?"

What kind indeed?

I shrug, determined to appear unaffected. "Probably an adult film star, or the child of circus folk. Hard to know."

Not that it matters. The woman could call herself Piggly Wiggly and the men would collapse at her feet. Half a dozen words from her ruby lips and the entire room falls under her spell. I swear, it's like watching some kind of magic trick, the way every set of eyes gravitate toward her, completely enchanted.

Down jealousy. Just because Ash is inking her doesn't mean he's fucking her. I'm sure he doesn't sleep with every single client.

Right?

God, I hate my brain sometimes. She's such a sadistic bitch.

Although, unless there are two women named Raven hanging around Black Lotus, this is the same woman Ash escorted to the wine bar earlier. On *my* recommendation.

Determined to get my brain on another track—any at this point—I grab a tablet off a nearby table and open Ash's portfolio before thrusting it under Mina's nose. "Have you seen Ash's work before?"

Mina shakes her head, flipping through a few photos. "You're not kidding. His designs are so realistic."

"Braden said Ash is the best in the business with portraits. It's like looking at a photograph."

"What do they call this style?" Mina asks, holding up a photo of an elderly man sitting in a rocking chair.

"Photorealism," Ash's voice rumbles behind me, right before his hand drifts down to palm my ass. "Excuse me, Little One."

I glance over my shoulder and give him a wink. "Excuse *you* is more like it."

"You love it." It's a declarative statement as his hand tightens ever so slightly, giving my peach a squeeze.

I turn to face him, crossing my arms over my chest as I arch a brow at him. "Do I, though? Thought I was tricky to read."

"For some people, but I've got a good handle on what makes you wet."

Holy shit, did he just announce that fact in front of Mina and the entire crowd gathered to watch him lay down ink?

And why do I love that concept so much?

I lift my hand, gliding one finger down the center of his chest. If he wants to play, we'll play. "Maybe you got lucky."

He grasps my finger, halting any further movement. "Maybe I'll get lucky again."

His voice rolls over me, setting every cell in my body on fire. Suddenly, words fail me as a flush climbs my cheeks.

Damn, but that sounds delightful.

"Although," Ash begins, shooting me a rueful smile as he rubs his jaw, "there is a change of plans later. Some friends surprised our shop with a catered party after the festival wraps."

So much for late night delights.

I wonder if his client, aka the inked goddess, is behind his itinerary change.

Still, I refuse to let on that it bothers me—much.

I force a smile and shrug. "Maybe you'll get lucky elsewhere, then. Maybe we *both* will. The night is young."

Yes, it's a cocky aside, but I've learned this is exactly how to handle men with egos the size of Asher Hammond's.

A gentle reminder that although he may possess a remarkably talented cock, he's not the only cock in town. Besides, he's partying with a bevy of women willing to do anything, and I mean *anything*, for a second of his attention.

It's not like he's missing out on opportunities tonight.

A fact I loathe more and more every second.

"Wait, a damn minute." Ash grabs my arm, sliding his hand down to grasp my fingers. "Um … why don't you come along? You'll have a good time. I guarantee it."

He shifts his weight and clears his throat, before averting his gaze to the far wall.

Oh, I know that maneuver well. It's one I've perfected over the years.

Asher Hammond, are you embarrassed? And … did you just ask me out?

After getting shot down twice by the man, I'm playing it safe. "Always a possibility."

I realize, a second too late, that I just used Ash's blow-off line against him.

A fact which is not lost on the man.

A scoff flies from his mouth. "I really don't like that response."

Time to turn the tables. I offer a slight shrug, knowing it will only further irk him. "Neither did I."

Ash leans in, his eyes darkening. "How about you try a different one? A better one."

My heart races in my chest, but I'm determined to play it cool. The less interested I appear, the more desperate he grows.

I like this version of the game.

I glance up at him, dragging my tongue along my lower lip. "Maybe? Is that good enough for you?"

"Not really."

Before I can kick off another sassy retort, Ash grabs me round the waist and hauls me into a small room off the main parlor floor.

"Are you locking me in the supply closet until I behave?" I ask, waving my hand at the shelves lined with towels, gloves, and an assortment of inks and bottles.

Ash backs me against the far wall, his muscled arms caging me in his embrace. "Something like that."

I dare to reach my hand up, tracing my finger along the scruff of his beard. "What can I do for you, *sir?*"

A low growl rises from his chest as he presses his body against mine. "Now, we're getting somewhere."

He slides his hand along my throat and tips my chin up before claiming my kiss. He swallows any arguments as his tongue slides against mine, his fingers holding me in the moment.

As if I'd look for an escape.

I rise on tiptoe, desperate to get closer, earning his grunt of approval as he knits his fingers in my hair.

His beard scrapes against my skin as our tongues tangle, his warm breath mingling with mine as the din outside fades away. There's a hunger in his kiss, as if he's reliving every delicious moment of our night together.

Ash slips his hands around my ass as he scoops me into his arms and guides my legs around his waist. "Fuck, but I missed you," he hisses, his breath hot against my neck.

Will I have sex in a supply closet, with a full house of patrons just on the other side of the door?

Not a doubt in my mind.

He bucks against me, his cock straining against his jeans as a guttural grunt escapes his throat.

Here's hoping he locked the door.

A second later, I get my answer, when Braden bursts into the closet.

"Hang on a second, Zane. Let me grab some towels." He stops dead in his tracks, shaking his head when he catches sight of us. "Seriously? Again? You two are worse than a couple of teenagers."

Oh. My. God.

Ash sets me down before shooting a dirty look at his brother. "How is it you always know just when to disturb me?"

"It's a supply closet. Use a bedroom next time." Braden chuckles, pulling a roll of towels off the shelf, before pivoting his gaze to me. "I must say, Ori, I never thought I'd see the day."

Then he leaves, not bothering to elaborate on his statement.

But there's no way I'm letting *that* one go.

I run a hand through my hair, certain Ash wrecked any semblance of a style during our exuberant, but short-lived, tryst. "What did Braden mean by that?"

Ash shrugs as he adjusts himself, his erection unmistakable beneath his jeans. "Who knows? Spouting shit, as usual. Isn't that what little brothers do?"

"I wouldn't know. He has terrible timing, though."

"Yes, he does." Ash drums the shelf with his fingers, skewing his mouth to the side in an adorable smirk as his gaze wanders over me. "I better get out there."

"Too bad I can't convince you to stay."

He gestures toward the pronounced bulge in his pants. "I'm sure you could, but I can't guarantee how long I'd remain in business."

I close the small distance between us, rising on tiptoe to steal a quick kiss. "But it would be so much fun."

Before he can reply, I yank open the door, fully aware of the half-dressed hussies watching me as I exit the supply closet with Ash close behind.

Am I sorry for ruining their afternoon? Not one iota.

Ash started it, and if Braden hadn't interrupted us, I sure as hell would have finished it.

Turning on my heel, I flash Ash a brilliant smile. "Have fun. Don't miss me too much."

But I know as I walk across the parlor, Ash's gaze hot on me, that he'll have one thing on his mind for the next few hours.

Me.

Chapter 15

The Fine Print of Flirtation

Ori

Mina has procured some prime real estate to watch the demonstration, no doubt in part because of her striking good looks. Even though she's dressed simply in a sweater and jeans, there is no denying the adoring glances shot her way.

Although, if any of them make an unwelcome advance, I'm breaking their fingers—along with other body parts.

Little big sister, at your service.

"Check you out," I state with a sly grin as I sidle up to my friend. "Even *I* can see from this vantage point."

"No doubt Ash would ensure you receive a front row seat." She pivots, her hands planted on her hips. "Are you still going to deny something is happening between you two?"

I turn my gaze forward, as a smile threatens to break across my face. "Absolutely."

"Your lipstick is smeared."

Shit.

Dragging a finger beneath my lip, I cast Mina a side-eye. "Better?"

She chuckles and shakes her head. "No."

With a huff, I throw up my hands in resignation. "Let me go fix my face. I'll be right back."

"Ash will only mess it up again." Another smirk dances its way across my friend's face. She's having *way* too much fun at my expense.

"Better stop or I'll have a chat with Braden."

The smile falls from her lips as her mouth drops open in a gape. "You wouldn't."

"Wouldn't I though?" I call the words out over my shoulder, before ducking into One More Page to fix my mussed appearance.

It's an empty threat, although part of me would love to speak to Braden about how amazing Mina is, and that he's a fool if he doesn't snatch her up immediately.

But Mina might bury me six feet under if I did that.

Right now, I have too many enjoyable moments in my future to take such a risk.

After fixing the smudge of lipstick barely noticeable under my lip—while simultaneously hoping Ash is wearing far more of it—I return to Black Lotus.

But something is different, or should I say, *someone*.

Mina stands rigid, her lips a thin line of disapproval.

"What's wrong?" I ask, pushing a lock of blonde hair away from her face. "Did someone say something to you? Whose ass do I need to kick?"

Mina shakes her head and offers a forced smile. "Everyone has been fine. Sweet, even. With one exception. *Her*."

I follow Mina's glare to Ash's client, Raven, the buxom, inky-haired beauty.

"What about her?"

"I don't like her. I don't like the way she's looking at Ash."

How can I respond to that statement? Hell, I hate it, too, but Ash is hardly virginal. Plus, he's gorgeous, so it's natural women will fawn over him.

Do I still loathe it? Of course. I am human, after all.

"She might stare at him, but she wasn't the one kissing him a few minutes ago." To be fair, I meant the words to stay in my head, and instantly regret the bevy of questions sure to follow my declaration.

Mina claps her hands together excitedly, her eyes dancing with amusement. "Ah, so you're finally admitting it."

"Worst kept secret in the world."

"Are you and Ash dating?"

I shake my head, waving my hands in tandem. "No. The man doesn't believe in the concept. He wanted to hang out tonight, but then some of his friends decided to throw a party in his honor. Screwed up all my plans for the evening."

"See? This is why I hate her," Mina reiterates, a scowl returning to her face.

"Don't count me out yet," I reply, straining to get a better view of Ash as he bends over to grab a towel from the floor. "I have ways of ensuring I get what I want."

Two large men squeeze in front of Mina and me, effectively blocking our view. Seems chivalry is dead with this duo.

Tugging Mina's sleeve, I use my slight size to my advantage, ducking around a few patrons and finding us a new spot with an even better line of sight.

It turns out this new spot has an added advantage: we're also now within earshot of Ash and his client.

Raven lounges on the tattoo bed, her ample breasts pressing into the leather surface and offering Ash an up close and personal view of her assets. Her legs kick lazily in the air, and she wiggles her ass every now and again, giving the rest of the patrons a thrill.

But her focus is singular.

Ash continues setting up his workstation, seemingly oblivious to the massive tits just inches from his nose. He motions for her to turn on her side and she obliges, ensuring her shapely stems are on full display, but Ash remains the consummate professional. He focuses on applying the custom stencil with polished precision, first smoothing it against her skin before peeling it back slowly.

Maybe, despite her obvious outward beauty, this woman is not a threat.

And maybe I'm the reason.

Raven glances over to where I'm standing, and a slow smile crosses her crimson lips. But it's not a friendly grin. It's the smile I imagine a viper would make before sinking its fangs into an unwitting victim.

"Branching out into new interests, I see." Raven speaks the words to Ash, but her gaze remains locked on me, aware I can hear every word.

Since Ash's back is to me, I can't see his expression, save for a slight shrug of his shoulders as he settles onto his stool. "What in the world does that mean?"

"Your little librarian. Is she a friend or a *friend?*"

Ash's chuckle rises into the air. "Cut that shit out and lie still before I screw up this design."

"You won't mess it up. You never do. But you didn't answer my question."

"Don't plan on it, either."

"You're no fun."

Ash keeps his focus on the tattoo, the steady buzz of the machine almost drowning out their conversation.

Almost.

Damn me and my supersonic hearing.

Raven huffs out a breath, pooching her lips in feigned annoyance. "Come on, tell me the truth. Who is she?"

"Why do you care?" Ash grumbles, keeping his hand steady as he lays down some ink.

"Because she's not your usual type, but you seem *mighty* interested in that one."

Now my ears really perk up, desperate to hear how Ash responds to her claim.

Yes, I'm thirty-nine years old, but deep down, I'm still just a girl with a heady crush.

Ash shakes his head as he wipes her design, another laugh rising from his chest. "Remember that woman I hated?"

"Your neighbor?"

Ash nods. "Turns out, I don't hate her after all."

I bite back a sarcastic laugh at his words.

Don't bowl me over with your romantic lines, Ash.

"Are they talking about you?" Mina asks, her voice a fierce whisper.

Why do people always pick the worst time to inject themselves into a conversation? Can't Mina see I'm busy eavesdropping?

"Shh." It's the only response my friend needs as she falls silent and I return my attention to the drama unfolding not five feet from me.

Raven wags her finger at Ash. "Wait a minute. She's the one you share a basement with, right?"

"One and the same."

"Did she sign the paperwork?"

"She did."

Raven shakes her head, a sly giggle escaping her lips. "*You* are devious."

Ash pauses again, tilting his head toward her. "What do you mean?"

"Now I get it. You, buttering her up and showering her with attention. Of course, you said you'd do *anything* to ensure that speakeasy opened. Well played, Ash. Well played."

He waves his hand, clearly distracted by her incessant questions. "You're reading too much into it. It's just … business. Nothing more than that."

Ash's words seep into my soul with the finality of a chainsaw cutting through wood.

I guess I'm nothing in his equation.

Raven leans over, one crimson nail dragging along his biceps. "And you are one hell of a talented businessman. Perhaps I can find a deal *we* can negotiate."

Ash's shoulders shake with silent laughter as he waves her hand away. "Will you please stop so I can concentrate?"

So glad they find this scenario funny.

Seems I'm the only one *not* laughing.

"Want to get out of here?" Mina asks, her glare fixed on Ash and his 'friend'.

I nod, keeping my eyes downcast. "Yeah. I've seen enough."

Actually, I've seen and heard *more* than enough.

Ash didn't insult me—at least not outright. He simply reaffirmed my initial belief that his change in attitude was just a facade. A means to an end.

Deep down, I always suspected that was Ash's true motive behind his flirtations.

Quite simple, really.

His recent behavior clearly hinges on his need for my signature. I'm not sure why he's still pretending to be interested, except to keep me in his pocket until the speakeasy opens.

Let's be honest, people have fucked for far more trivial reasons. That's what the rational side of my brain tells me.

But my emotions? That's another story entirely. I believed his words, the look in his eyes, the desire in his kiss. I believed they were meant for me because I was different.

Turns out, I'm nothing more than a business transaction.

The emotional side of my psyche is tempted to grab a tattoo machine and decorate both their faces with chicken-scratch designs.

We'll see who's laughing then.

Before I can slip through the crowd and return to the safety of my bookstore, Ash looks over, catching my eye. A strange expression flits across his face, as he no doubt wonders which parts of his conversation I overheard.

Or perhaps he couldn't care less.

What matters right now is *I* do.

Ash sets his machine down and crooks his finger at me.

I have two choices: ignore him or be an adult and talk to the man.

Have I mentioned how much it sucks being an adult?

I pull off my glasses and pinch the bridge of my nose, desperate to calm the anger brewing inside me.

Then, with a quick glance at Mina, I trudge the few steps to where Ash sits.

Ash drums the table, his green eyes intent on my face. "Where are you running off to? I'm just getting started."

Better question, Ash, why do you care?

I shrug and tilt my head toward the exit. "My employees need their break. Don't want to become known as the grinch who killed their Christmas spirit."

Ash chuckles, running a hand over his jaw. "Why would they ever think that?"

Are we really reverting to small talk? "If they'd spoken to you, they'd have thought far worse."

His eyes darken as they sweep over my form. "Not if they spoke to me in the last week. You're the gift that keeps on giving."

No wonder the man can juggle a dozen women at the same time. He possesses an uncanny ability to make you feel like you're the only woman he sees, even in a room packed with potential dates.

One hell of a schtick.

Too bad it no longer works on me.

An annoyed grunt escapes my lips. Not technically a response, but Ash picks up on my hostile demeanor. Why wouldn't he? It was my *only* personality trait around him for those first six months. Guess I got it right the first time.

"Well, come back over when you're done." Ash jerks his

thumb toward Raven, who's watching our interaction with a great deal of interest. "You know where I'll be."

At least until he's finished tattooing his 'friend'. Then my money is on any number of hotel rooms in the area. Or perhaps he'll give her a private tour of the basement—if he hasn't already.

"Inking your Jessica Rabbit-Snow White mashup," I mutter under my breath, the words meant solely for my benefit—and ego.

Apparently, Ash also possesses supersonic hearing. He throws his head back and laughs, a full-on, full body laugh that reverberates through the surrounding air. "That might be the most accurate description ever. I'll have to let Raven know your nickname for her."

Wrong response, Asher Hammond.

"I'm sure you will." I bite out the words, my jaw tight with aggravation.

Not that Raven will care. The woman has zero hangups about her feminine wiles. Just ask any man in Black Lotus and they'll agree.

But she's got her eye on the grand prize and no doubt, the feeling is mutual.

I'm not a threat by any stretch.

She probably sees me in the same way Ash does, as a pretty and uptight geeky woman with zero ink, no piercings, and a preference for jazz clubs over nightclubs.

Seems me and my wickedly talented mouth will have to find another venue in which to play.

This one is all booked up.

"Did I hear my name mentioned?" Raven's pale arm wraps around Ash's shoulder as she interjects herself into our chat.

How lovely. This afternoon keeps getting better and better.

"What were you two saying about me?" she asks, shooting Ash a coy smile.

"Talking about your ink and the party later." Thankfully, Ash doesn't divulge my nickname for the black-haired beauty. Maybe he's saving it for when they're alone so he can claim it as his own.

Whatever works.

"Are you coming, too?" Raven inquires, arching a sculpted brow at me.

"We'll see," I mumble. "It depends on how I feel later. The shop is busy, so I'll likely be too tired."

Code for no chance in hell.

"That's a shame." Her voice is soft, but there's no missing the tone—dripping with sarcasm, layered beneath a breathy whisper. "We haven't officially met. I'm Raven."

"I heard." After a beat, I huff out a sigh and extend my hand. "I'm Ori."

"The bookstore owner." A smile lights up her face as her gaze volleys between Ash and me. "You look like a bookstore owner."

Now what the fuck is that supposed to mean?

Raven catches the anger flashing across my face and rests a hand on my arm. "It's not an insult. You've got this adorable librarian aesthetic about you."

Shoot me. Now.

There's nothing as humbling as a gorgeous vixen calling you adorable. Bonus points for doing it in front of the man who used me—not for sex, but for my signature.

I feel like a Pomeranian.

Wearing glasses.

About to turn feral.

Sure, call me adorable, Ms. Thirst Trap. We'll see how that plays out for you when I rip those extensions out by the root.

And … yep. Now I'm feral.

It's time to go.

"I have to get back to work, as do you. See you around, Ash." A choked laugh emerges from my throat, but it's the best I can manage.

"Hey," Ash cuts in, forcing me to pivot in his direction once more. "Are you coming back?"

What I want to do is scream at him that I'd far rather endure a root canal sans Novocain. But being the prim and proper librarian geek that I am, I refrain from causing a scene.

Besides, this is his shop and if Raven knows the truth of Ash's motives with me, most of these people do, too.

To be brutally honest, I'm too damn embarrassed by that notion to raise a fuss.

I thought Ash saw me. Turns out, all he saw was a means to an end, and I fell for it.

"Who knows, Ash? It's anybody's guess."

I don't stick around to hear his response. There's nothing he can say to make this situation suck any less.

Mina waits for me at the door of Black Lotus, her foot tapping out an erratic rhythm.

Trust me, I feel you, my friend.

"You heard?" I ask, although I already know the answer. Anger wafts off her in waves and despite her doll-like appearance, I've no doubt Mina could kick some serious ass when provoked.

Annabelle and the feral Pomeranian, reporting for duty.

"What a bitch," she snaps, narrowing her gaze at Raven. "What does he see in her, anyway?"

"Tits, ass, and a good time. Besides, she's right. I am a mousy librarian type, and you know what? I like me, just as I am. Fuck him and her if they don't appreciate it. Better yet, they can fuck each other and leave me out of it."

Mina's mouth drops open at my forceful reply. Too bad I don't have the guts to say it to their faces. "Damn straight, but do you actually mean those words?"

I blink back tears as we duck from the shop and into the shared hallway. But instead of allowing the weight of my feelings to kowtow me, I straighten and roll my shoulders back.

"Without a doubt. He can have his basement and his lies. I'll keep my heart and pride intact. There are plenty of great men out there. Too bad Asher Hammond isn't one of them."

"Want me to mop the floor with them? Trip over something while he's tattooing her and screw up her ink?"

I fiddle with the ring on my hand and force a tremulous smile. "Here I thought *my* mind was traveling some dubious roads today. No, leave them alone. It's not a big deal."

Or should I say, *I'm* not a big deal, at least not according to Ash. No, to him, I'm nothing.

Mina wraps an arm around me, offering a hug of solidarity.

She knows I'm lying, but she'll let me play my part.

Suck it up, Oriana. One pitfall of being a romantic is falling for a man who can fake affection as easily as he fakes a smile.

Chapter 16

The Lines We Cross

Ash

"Ash, you are a work of art," Raven muses, admiring the fresh ink adorning her hip.

I set my tattoo machine aside and shake out my hands. Four hours of precision work have taken a toll on my digits, although the result so far is a masterpiece. "Not even close, but that beauty will be."

To be fair, it may be one of my best pieces and it's not even finished. But the outline is perfection. Two ravens perch atop a wrought-iron gate, with thorny vines twisting through the rails, spelling out the word Unbreakable. Roses curve between the thorns, the black and grays popping against Raven's ivory skin.

Just wait until I add the hints of color throughout the piece on her next session. This one is definitely headlining my portfolio.

"Your skin took the color beautifully," I murmur, before placing a protective bandage over the design. "You know the drill—wash with a gentle soap, pat dry, apply a thin layer of ointment and avoid the sun."

Raven chuckles and shoots me a flirty grin. "Do I look like I spend much time in the sun?"

"No, you're pretty much vampire status."

"Good thing you like vampires."

I ignore her heated reply and focus on massaging my palms with my thumbs, trying to ease the stiffness that's taken up residence. My hands ache, but it's a small price to pay for creating art.

There are two things I love in this world—tattooing and sex. Some may call me arrogant, but I worked my ass off to master my skill, and it's way more than pushing a needle into flesh. I listen to my clients. I hear their stories—a random collection of the best and worst moments of their lives—before guiding them to a piece of art that encapsulates that moment.

And watching someone release a long-held toxic belief or trauma after gazing upon their new skin art? There's no better feeling in the world.

Except for sex.

Not just any sex, either. The kind of raucous love-making that turns you inside out and leaves you ravenous for more.

Great sex is hard to come by. Knock-down, run-you-over-like-a-steam-engine sex? Even more rare, and there have only been two women to drive my mind over the ledge like that.

One ripped my heart apart years ago and the other—Ori—never returned tonight.

Even though my focus remained on Raven's tattoo, I shot numerous glances at the people gathered around my workstation, hoping my petite brunette neighbor would be hanging out in the crowd. There's something about her presence that's warm and inviting. As crazy as it sounds, I feel safe knowing she's nearby.

I also feel an overwhelming need to rip her clothes off, but that's hardly surprising after the night we spent together. Let's put it this way: if Braden hadn't burst into the supply closet, I would have torn Ori's pants down and licked her sweet pussy until she couldn't stand. Hell, I was tempted to do it even after he discovered our hiding spot. Why not give the good patrons of Black Lotus one hell of a show?

But Ori didn't come back, and I don't believe her story about One More Page being *that* busy.

No, she practically ran out of here, all thanks to Raven and her backhanded compliment.

In Raven's defense, her comment about Ori is dead-on-balls accurate. She *does* have an adorable bookish look about her, an air of innocence that covers a brilliant and dirty mind. Not to mention an incredibly delicious set of curves.

What that little librarian fails to realize is her effect on the male population.

Oriana Thorne is fucking beautiful, and she has no idea how many men around this town lust after her.

But after paying close attention over the last week, I do, and it's too damn many.

These guys think they're slick, as they peruse the shelves of her store and ask questions about books they'll never read, all the while dropping hints about how they'd love to show her around Sparkwood.

They find a reason to linger outside the shop or by the coffee bar, hoping they might say something witty enough to whet Ori's appetite.

I've yet to see one succeed in scoring a date, but I've watched it play out on five separate occasions.

With one particularly dedicated would-be suitor, I strolled outside Black Lotus and leaned against the front glass window, my arms crossed over my chest as I fixed him with a look of death. Sometimes, words aren't necessary—he heard me loud and clear.

Look, Ori's a tiny woman. It's my duty to protect her from the undesirables around here. Even if in her mind, *I'm* the most undesirable one at the moment.

Something I plan to remedy just as soon as I finish cleaning up.

Zane pokes his head into the studio space and flashes an admiring grin at Raven. "Locking up now. You two ready to go?"

"We'll catch up with you," Raven replies for both of us, as she bends over to pull on her heels, offering us a view of her plump ass.

That adage about when you've got it, flaunt it, works double time with a woman like Raven. What God didn't give her, a plastic surgeon supplied, and she's more than happy to work every angle of her physique.

Guess that's why she's one of the hottest adult film stars in the industry. I can claim I didn't watch her flicks after meeting her the first time, but why lie? Plus, I didn't have to look up a damn thing—Zane gladly offered to wrangle up some video evidence. Let's just say the woman has some serious moves, one in particular that involves some rope, a chandelier, and plenty of candle wax.

I'll leave you to fill in the blanks.

And I know Raven's end game, at least for tonight. She flirted incessantly with me during our session, even allowing her blouse to slip low enough to reveal one pert, pierced nipple.

Subtle, she is not.

It's not the first time, either. When she visited Black Lotus to commission her custom piece, she dropped numerous hints about us spending some quality time together.

No doubt where her head is at, now that we're both off duty.

Zane gives the doorframe a light smack, a smirk crossing his face as he shoots me a look that says I'm the luckiest man alive right now. "Guess I'll see you two later … or not."

Then he's gone, leaving me alone with porn's hottest commodity.

"I need to book another session, but you better not make me wait too long," Raven says as she leans against the wall, her lips curved in a pouty smile. "You're addictive, Ash. I think I'll need several more rounds with you."

Quite the compliment, considering I've yet to show Raven *any* of my talents beyond tattooing.

Tugging a hand through my hair, I slide my machine into its case and thumb the latch closed. "Book yourself a slot anytime. Can't wait to finish that piece. You're happy now? Just wait until I'm done."

Here's the thing: I didn't mean my reply to sound sexual. Honest to fucking God.

But the second the words leave my lips, I realize that's exactly how she's going to take it.

"You read my mind. How about we slot in time tonight? See how happy we can make each other?"

I chuckle and click my tongue against my teeth. There

it is. I wondered how long it would take her to lay it out there.

A week ago, I'd have been all over her plan for extracurricular activities.

But that was before my tiny neighbor turned my world upside down, even though I'd sooner die than admit that fact aloud. So long as I keep it stashed in the recesses of my brain, I'm safe.

More importantly, my heart is.

Still, I invited Ori to the party tonight. There's no way I could—or would—desert her to copulate with Raven in an adjoining room.

That would be rude.

Now, taking Ori into a private area to defile her delicious body all night? That is *high* on my list of priorities.

"Well?" Raven crosses the small space, giving me a slight hip check.

I pull my jacket from the hook, nodding toward the door. "Actually, I'm bringing someone to the party, so I'll meet you there."

A low laugh rises from her chest as she waves her hand at me. "Let me guess. Your little librarian? Don't give me that look. We both know I'm right."

"I have no idea what you're talking about," I reply with feigned innocence.

Raven smirks and reaches up to wipe her finger along my lip. "Really? So, you two just like wearing matching lipstick?"

I drag a hand over my mouth and chuckle. "Thanks for waiting four hours to tell me."

Now she's staring at me, her arms crossed over her

chest, as if waiting for me to dig myself in deeper. "You're not denying it, either. Damn, you really like her."

Her words hit me like a jolt of electricity. I've been accused of many things over the years, but falling for a woman isn't one of them. At least not since Lucille.

If Raven can read my emotions this easily, then everyone else can, too.

Time to play it off like it's nothing, because that's all it is.

A harmless flirtation. Some sexually charged moments. A few delicious memories of one delectable woman.

A woman I can't get out of my damn brain.

I force a smile, shrugging off her statement. "Come on, Raven, you know me. It's just a little fun. Nothing more to it than that. She's just a friend."

The second the words leave my mouth, I realize I'm trying harder to convince myself than her.

And neither of us is buying it.

"A beautiful friend," Raven adds.

"She *is* beautiful." Along with sexy, smart, and absolutely incredible in bed.

Raven grabs her purse and releases a noisy sigh. "Three is a fun number, too, although something tells me you don't plan on sharing Ori with anyone."

She's right, on all counts. Threesomes are a ton of fun, and I've no doubt Raven's libido would wear both Ori and me out, but this time, I'm not game for the game.

Ori is everything I want. For tonight, at least.

Must keep reminding myself of that, before I do something *really* stupid, like fall for her.

"Never was big on sharing."

"At least not where Ori is concerned. Am I right?"

Raven doesn't wait for me to answer. "Oh well, looks like I'll have to find someone else to adore me tonight."

I motion toward the exit with a smile. "You won't have any trouble. There's always a line of men desperate for you."

"But I wanted *you*, and you had to ruin it by developing a crush. Bastard." She pivots in front of the door, her red lips once again curved in a teasing grin. "Let's make a deal. I'll be back in Sparkwood next month for my follow-up session, and then you are taking me to dinner. I deserve a fair shot, too, and knowing your storied history, you'll have moved on to the next woman by then."

No doubt about it, Raven is the female version of me. She works hard and plays harder, but her heart never gets involved. She gets my motives and respects my boundaries.

On paper, she's perfect for me. No strings, no entanglements. Just good, dirty fun.

But life doesn't exist on paper and my current reality orbits around a different woman. Although Raven is likely correct that I'll be past any lingering feelings for Ori within the next few weeks.

Crush or no crush.

But until that happens, I need to maintain my distance from other women.

"See you next month," I answer with a smile.

"Goodnight, gorgeous man. Have fun tonight." She presses a kiss to my mouth before exiting the building, her hips swaying as she walks to her sports car.

I lock the door behind her, my foot tapping out an erratic rhythm as she drives away.

"Interesting decision," I mutter under my breath. "I need a drink."

But that's not true. What I need is to see Ori and pick up where our earlier tryst in the closet left off. Except maybe this time, we'll play around in *her* store.

After a last glance around my shop, I cross the connecting hallway to One More Page, noting the darkened interior.

At least all the customers are gone, which means there's nothing holding Ori and me back from playtime, a fact which makes my dick harden in anticipation.

Fuck, what she does to me.

With a quick adjustment and a grunt, I knock on the door.

Mina appears a moment later, her face sullen when she sees me on the other side of the etched glass. She pulls the door open, her fingers drumming the doorjamb. "What's up?"

"I'm here for Ori. She around?"

"Not for you, she isn't."

Chapter 17

All Roads Lead to Her

Ash

*S*omeone is not in a good mood.

I wait for a beat, assuming Mina will spill some additional details about her boss's whereabouts, but she remains silent, her eyes narrowed in aggravation.

"Do you know where she is?"

Mina shrugs. "Yes."

Okay, I'm done with this schoolyard game.

"Mina, where the hell is Ori?"

She rubs her brow, releasing a noisy sigh. "She went home."

Now we're getting somewhere. "Perfect. How about you give me her address and I'll get out of your way. I'm sure you're beat after the festival today."

Yes, I throw in the last bit for effect, because I've never seen Mina so hostile toward me and I know I have done nothing to provoke her.

"She's not going to that party, so you might as well head over there alone. Not that you'll stay that way for long."

Mina mutters the last sentence through gritted teeth, and it hits me I'm in the doghouse.

For what, I'm not entirely sure.

But I'm getting a bit tired of Mina serving as a sentry to her boss.

Crossing my arms over my chest, I clear my throat and swallow back the biting comment on the tip of my tongue. "What the hell am I missing here?"

Mina pulls the door open and waves me inside. I trail her to the front counter, where she pulls out her phone and dials a number. "Ori? Ash would like to speak with you. Hang on."

Then she thrusts the phone in my direction before walking to the back of the store.

"Thank you," I call after her, a low chuckle rising from my chest. Seems Mina needs a drink more than I do. "Hey, Ori."

"Hey yourself."

Damn, I love this woman's voice—the way it wraps around every syllable, leaving a cloud of sparks, just like her tongue left sparks on my skin. "About this party tonight—"

But Ori doesn't let me finish my statement. "Yeah, after thinking it over, I decided against going. But have a great time. Thanks for asking me to tag along."

Her words, by themselves, are innocuous, but it's the tone that puts me on edge—sharp and to the point, as that honeyed whisper quickly morphs into a serrated knife.

Determined to lighten the mood, I laugh. "Did you find something better to do?"

"Yes."

That one word, that single syllable dismissing our plans, sends my temper into the danger zone.

"I thought we were hanging out tonight," I reply, desperate to wrangle my anger.

"I changed my mind."

What the hell? I pace the area near the counter, my steps falling heavy against the floor. "Were you planning on telling me this or just standing me up?"

"It's not like you asked me on a date, Ash. You and your friends will party until the wee hours of the morning. Sorry I don't find that appealing. Besides, you really think you'd have a good time if you were stuck entertaining me all evening instead of ... hanging out with them?"

"Didn't answer my question." Not that it matters. She's given me the blow-off. I should let it lie and walk away, knowing Ori and I are a terrible idea.

But I can't do that. Not yet anyway.

Because I was in that closet with her, and I felt her heart racing as I held her close. Tasted the desire on her skin as my mouth claimed her.

You can't fake that. And we *both* felt it.

I can't be wrong again. Not about this.

That thought careens my brain back to Lucille once more, and the way she played me for a fool. The way she walked away without bothering to ask if I could survive without her.

Most days, those memories remain safely under lock and key, but Ori's sudden one-eighty has brought them all to the forefront—along with a bevy of emotions I swore I'd never endure again.

Ori's voice cuts into my thoughts, only a tinge softer than before. "I'm not sure what question you think I'm avoiding."

"If you're not spending time with me, what *are* you doing tonight?"

"Nothing special."

Oh, this conversation is swiftly moving from bad to worse.

"You're skipping out on hanging out with me to do nothing special? That's pretty messed up, no?"

Ori sighs into the phone. "That's not how I meant it. I'm exhausted and I would be a terrible addition to a party. Trust me, you'll have much more fun without me."

This keeps getting better and better.

Now, she's covering her tracks in a desperate attempt to soften the blow. But I learned ten years ago to leave any place—or person—where I'm not wanted, and it's apparent Oriana Thorne just joined that list.

Proof positive that falling for someone, in *any* capacity, is a horrible idea.

And now, my ego is the only thing I'm concerned with saving. "Trust me, I *will* have fun. Don't you worry about that. It will be a night to remember."

Do I sound like a pompous asshole? Absolutely, but I have every right. The woman I was planning to blow everyone else off for just blew me off—to do nothing special.

I rate below nothing special on her scale and I'm going to make damn sure she never rates on *any* scale of mine again.

Damn it, I hate this feeling. I swore I'd never come back here and now, here I stand, neck deep in it. Questioning what I said or did, or didn't say or do, that turned Ori from my late-night dessert into a desert of feelings.

Screw this shit.

I'm moving on, starting now.

With a grunt, I toss Mina's phone onto the counter and storm from the shop. Time for some liquid amber to soothe my frazzled nerves and pride, and I know just where Ori stashed that bottle of single malt.

Sue me, now I *really* need a drink. I'll buy the woman a fresh bottle.

My boots echo against the basement stairs as I beeline for the whiskey. Then I take a swig and settle on the edge of the couch, my eyes perusing the dingy interior.

Hard to believe in a few months, this place will morph into my decades long dream—a little slice of the glitzy '20s right here in Sparkwood.

I should be thrilled, right? This is what I've always wanted and here it is, within reach.

But everything is different now, ever since that fateful night with Ori.

A night she doesn't care to remember and one I can't seem to forget.

What the hell happened? Is she *that* mad about Raven's comment? Enough to send me packing, too? It's not like Raven called Ori a hideous toad. Besides, Ori is a smart woman. Damn smart. There's no way she looks in a mirror and sees anything but a petite beauty staring back at her.

And if she hadn't blown me off, I would have spent the night reassuring her of just how fucking desirable she is.

But she has *nothing special* to do, and that was more appealing than time with me.

A quick glance at my phone tells me the party is rocking and rolling at the hotel. I can hop on my hog and be there in thirty minutes. Within the hour, I can be balls deep in Raven, as we create our own porn drama.

The woman is the stuff of legends and let's be honest, I have a similar reputation for providing pleasure.

Another sip of whiskey slides down my throat as my foot taps against the floor in an erratic beat.

I've earned a damn party and a happy ending. Raven wants to give me both with no strings attached. No promises of dinner and commitment the next morning.

It's perfect. Surface level pleasure.

Because who needs Oriana Thorne's company, right?

Not me.

Still …

"Fuck," I groan, tugging a hand through my hair.

Home. Party. Home. Party.

Guaranteed sex or guaranteed sleepless night.

How is this even a question circling my brain?

"Oriana, you really are a damn siren."

I take a final swallow from the bottle before tucking it back on the shelf. Time to get out of here.

My foot is on the first step when the door from the hallway yanks open, sending a shaft of light streaming into the basement.

Mina stands at the top of the stairs, arms crossed over her chest, that same belligerent expression coloring her features.

Seriously, woman, I am not in the mood.

"What's up, Mina?"

"A woman is here, looking for you. She was banging on the door to Black Lotus as I was leaving. Said she needs to speak with you immediately."

"Wonderful," I mutter. "Did you get her name?"

"My name is Jade, and you'd better not claim to be too

busy for me." My cousin steps from the shadows wearing a wide grin.

"Jade, what the hell are you doing here?" I ask, rushing up the stairs to enfold her into a bear hug. "It's been forever."

"Tell me about it," Jade giggles, pressing a noisy kiss to my cheek.

I pivot and catch sight of Mina, who is now glaring holes into me. "Mina, this is Jade—my cousin."

The fury brewing on Mina's face slides away, replaced by a genuine smile. "Oh, I thought you were—"

"One of his many women?" Jade jokes as she shakes Mina's hand. "No, although I fought quite a few of them off back in the day."

"Nice to meet you." Mina turns her attention to me, the smile wavering. "I have something for you."

"Okay." This should be interesting. "Jade, give me a second? I'll be right back."

I follow Mina into One More Page, wondering if I'm about to receive a second earful on my life choices.

Let me tell you, I'm a patient man, but after tonight, it's wearing damn thin. And being cajoled by a twenty-five-year-old might be the tipping point.

"What's up?" I ask.

"Ori just called."

Did she now?

I lock my arms across my chest and cock a brow at the tall blonde. It's my standard, 'this had better be good' stance. "And?"

Mina grabs a book from the shelf and holds it out toward me. "She was researching books about speakeasies and found one she thought was perfect. It was a special order, and it arrived yesterday. She wanted you to have it."

I take the book from her outstretched hand, noting the colorful tabs littering random pages. "What's all this?"

Mina shrugs. "Ori went through it and tabbed the areas she thought might interest you. Certain styles and interiors she liked, and thought would be a good fit for your bar."

Talk about an unexpected—and contradictory—development. She wants to help me, but she doesn't want to be around me.

It doesn't make any damn sense.

"Did Ori read the book already?"

"Yeah. That's how she spent last night—curled up in bed with your book. Then again, isn't that typical of a librarian type?"

A whispered curse flies from my mouth. Now we're getting somewhere. I surmised Ori was angry about Raven's statement, but I didn't think she took it *that* hard.

One thing Oriana seems to possess in spades is gumption and a healthy self-confidence, which flies in the face of Mina's intimation.

I meet Mina's sky-colored gaze, noting the anger bubbling in their depths. Have to love how much she defends and protects her friend.

Come to think of it, I'm damn protective of Ori, too. Even if that's the last thing Mina believes.

Running a hand over my brow, I heave out a sigh. "Your boss is a gorgeous woman."

"Absolutely."

"Raven's comment wasn't meant to insult her. Hell, she thinks Ori is hot as hell. We both do."

"Come on, don't play dumb. You and I both know your

friend meant it as an insult. More importantly, Ori knows that, too."

I reach out and grasp Mina's sleeve. "Hey, I'll talk to Ori and get this all straightened out."

"Does it matter?" Mina shoves her hat on her head before tugging her keys from her pocket. "You got what you wanted."

And once again, my back is up. "What does that mean?"

Mina turns and releases a noisy breath. "The speakeasy, Ash. The reason behind *all of this*."

All of what? And then it dawns on me.

"Hey, Ash, are you about done?" Jade breaks into my conversation, her head peeking through the bookstore door.

"You'd better go. Besides, I'm tired and want to go home," Mina replies, walking toward the exit.

But I need Mina to understand that the speakeasy, although the catalyst in my situation with Ori, is not the reason I'm still hanging around.

I need her to know … actually, I have no idea what to tell her because I don't know what I'm feeling, and let's be honest, I need to have this chat with Ori, not her employee.

Mina locks the door to One More Page before brushing past me down the shared hallway, her steps graceful even in clunky winter boots.

"Mina," I call to her, waiting until she pauses at the exterior door. "That's not why."

"You sure about that? Goodnight, Ash."

Scrubbing my face with my hand, I release an aggravated huff as the door falls closed and Mina heads toward her car.

At least now I'm getting to the crux of the issue, the real reason behind Ori's icy facade.

She thinks I used her. Fucked her to get her on board with the speakeasy.

It's a given that women think differently about sex than men. Most men would be fine with a gorgeous woman using them for a good time. Hell, I know I'm fine with the concept.

Or I am with *most* women.

But then there's Ori, and it's more than how amazing she is in bed and how perfect her body feels next to mine.

When she blew me off tonight, the first emotion I felt was jealousy, that another guy somewhere was getting what belonged to me. Standard emotion, with one caveat: I don't get jealous.

It's not that I think I'm so great or irreplaceable. Trust me, I've had my ego knocked down enough times to know that's a crock of shit. And I guarantee there were a plethora of women in my past who used me for a myriad of reasons: payback, revenge, reassurance they were desirable—the list goes on and on.

But I didn't care either way. Whether I saw them the next day or never again, it didn't matter.

Until Ori.

I need to stay away from her. That's the safest route. Return to my previous life and move ahead as scheduled.

I have a choice to make—let things lie as they are and allow Ori to believe what she wants about me and our night together or patch things up, thereby entering unknown territory with a woman for the first time in a decade.

Both ideas scare the shit out of me.

"Ash?"

Jade's voice cuts into my internal monologue, and I shoot her a rueful smile. "Sorry. Got a lot on my mind."

"So I heard. You're opening the speakeasy. That's amazing. I can't wait to see it."

"You're on the VIP list."

She laughs. "I damn well better be. Don't make me call your folks and pull the family card."

"What are you doing here, anyway?"

Jade motions toward the parking lot. "I was out with a friend, and we got into an argument, so I bailed. But since he drove, I was without wheels. Can you give me a lift?"

"Do I need to kick someone's ass?"

"Not unless you want to kick mine." She shrugs and sighs. "I was a bit of a bitch, and I'll apologize to him tomorrow. Tonight, I'd like to forget about it and walking three miles while freezing my ass off isn't the way to accomplish that feat."

"Can't imagine it would be therapeutic for your mood." Lifting the book, I gesture toward Black Lotus. "Let me put this inside and grab the spare helmet."

"What's that? A gift from one of your adoring fans?"

Dear cousin, if you only knew.

An embarrassed chuckle escapes my lips as I run a hand over my beard. "Not exactly. It's from Ori. She owns the bookstore. It's all about the Roaring '20s and speakeasy culture."

"She tabbed sections for you, too?" Jade shoots me a knowing grin. "Someone has a crush. How very odd for you."

An hour ago, I would have agreed with my cousin, but now I realize I'm probably deeper into feelings than Ori at this point.

And that is *not* a place I enjoy being.

I brush off her comment and duck into Black Lotus to grab the helmet. I pause by my office but decide against leaving the book. For some dumb reason, I want to keep it with me, thumb through the noted pages, and see the world through Ori's eyes.

When I stroll back out, Jade chuckles and points to the book before putting the helmet on her head. "Change your mind?"

"I'm taking it home." After stowing it safely in my saddlebag, I hop on the bike and glance at my cousin, still standing on the sidewalk.

But she's not budging, and neither is her Cheshire Cat grin, visible even through the helmet.

"What?" I ask, rolling my eyes.

"Looks like someone does have a crush, and that someone is *you*."

"Get on or I'm letting your happy ass walk home."

Jade settles behind me, clasping her arms about my waist. "Deny it all you want, but I've known you since you were in diapers. I know all of Asher Hammond's deep, dark secrets."

"Are you done busting my balls?"

"Almost. One last thing. I want to meet Ori."

I turn slightly, a perplexed look on my face. "Why?"

"Because she's got you twisted up in knots, and I never thought I'd see that happen. I want to hug the woman for breaking the impenetrable wall around your heart."

"It's not like that with her," I argue, although I'm not entirely sure what it is anymore.

"Oh yes, it is. It's exactly like that, but I'd fix whatever you messed up before she slips through your fingers."

"For your information, an adult film star invited me to a private party tonight. One of the biggest stars in the business."

My piss poor attempt to throw my cousin off my scent is futile.

"Thanks for proving my point," she laughs.

"How did I do that?"

"The world's biggest porn star invites you to a party and you're going home to bed alone. Tell me I'm wrong."

"Whatever," I mutter, starting the bike and easing onto the street.

But the truth is, I can't deny Jade's claim.

And I'm not sure that I want to.

Chapter 18

A Jump Start and a False Start

Ori

"Are you getting your happy little ass down here soon?"

I bite back a smile at Roger's aggravated tone, considering our dinner plans aren't for another twenty minutes. "Do you miss me or something?"

"That's beside the point. The hostess has been shooting me dirty looks for the last ten minutes. She likely thinks my dinner guest is a figment of my imagination."

"Not a far reach. Isn't James with you?"

"He couldn't make it. Another bullshit late-night meeting. You know how those Wall Street types are."

James accepted a high-level position a few months back, and although the money and prestige are nice, Roger is growing weary of his husband being MIA all the time.

That's why he takes advantage of his now ample free time to visit me in Sparkwood. It gets his mind off his marriage woes and out of the city for a bit.

Plus, I get to spend time with my dear friend. It's a win-win situation and trust me, I need a few of those.

"Give me ten minutes, and I'll be there."

"Starting … now."

He clicks off the line and I toss my phone into my bag, grateful my buddy is in town again.

I need some fun and laughter, because the last week has been anything but enjoyable, and it's all Asher Hammond's fault.

"Fuck him," I mutter, jabbing my key into the ignition. "Or rather, not."

But when I turn the key, nothing happens.

After three more attempts, I realize it's not my truck's sadistic attempt at a joke.

"You have to be kidding me," I mutter, resting my head against the steering wheel and trying without success to force my truck's engine to turn over through sheer willpower.

Nope, not happening.

It's dead as a doornail, and to make matters worse, it's almost dark and Main Street stands practically deserted—with one exception.

Black Lotus is hopping tonight.

I guarantee at least one guy in there owns a set of jumper cables.

But that means I have to walk into Black Lotus and possibly see or speak to Asher Hammond, which is something I've avoided the last few days.

I'll admit that it's juvenile behavior, but my bruised ego doesn't give a damn.

Look, I know I'm pretty and smart. I refuse to play coy and act like I have no clue men find me attractive.

But Ash's friend Raven made me feel like a gangly teenager all over again—awkward limbs, no tits, and thick glasses—standing in stark contrast to her sculpted perfection.

Not that Mother Nature has much to do with her current silhouette. Oh no, she's seen the inside of a plastic surgeon's office more than once.

That petty thought would have been enough to maintain my equilibrium until she opened her mouth—again—and intimated I was a destination fuck for Ash.

Basically, he screwed me to reach his desired destination. And it worked—hook, line and sinker.

That is the trouble in playing with playboys. You believe you're different only to learn you're just like all the rest.

We all want to be the exception, but with Asher Hammond, that isn't an option. You're one of many—take it or leave it.

I mouth a silent prayer and turn the key one more time. Maybe the gods will smile on me.

Or … maybe not.

With a grunt, I push open the truck door and walk into Black Lotus. A few heavily inked patrons glance over from their perch on the couch when I enter before returning their attention to the television.

"Hey Ori, what's up? Don't tell me you have an appointment." Braden walks over, wiping his hands on a paper towel.

I smile up at him. "No, but I do have a favor to ask."

"Anything for you."

He's such a cutie. Why couldn't I have a crush on him?

Ah, right, because that would make my life easier, and I have sworn an unspoken oath to never allow that to happen.

"My truck is dead, and I need a jump. I figured one of you might have jumper cables."

Braden glances out the window and nods. "No problem. Give me five minutes and I'll be right out."

"Take your time."

There's no sign of Ash as I cast a quick glance about the place. Better that way since I get all flustered, flushed, and stupid when I'm around that man.

Just like every other woman in town.

The man probably has a stack of deeds and presents a mile high, and all it costs him is a sexy smirk and a few hours of playtime.

How difficult his life must be.

I return to my truck and grab my phone. Time to catch up on some doomsday scrolling—*anything* to get my mind off the tatted man who turned my world upside down. A dose of online petty grievances feels like the perfect distraction.

A knock at my driver's side window damn near sends me through the roof and I pitch my phone across the truck's interior before my brain catches up, reminding me that Braden said he'd be out in a few minutes.

"Shit. Braden, you scared me the hell out of me." Placing my hand on my chest, I release a heavy sigh and glance over. "You're not Braden."

Ash grins and shakes his head. "Thanks for noticing. I hear you're having some car trouble, Little One. Pop the hood."

I hate Ash's nickname for me. Okay, to be fair, I love it, but I hate that I'm likely one of dozens of women with that assigned moniker.

I do as requested before jumping out of the truck,

burrowing my face into my coat to ward off the evening chill. "Question."

"Answer."

"Isn't that your bike over there?" I point toward the shiny chrome beast parked in front of Black Lotus.

Ash shoots the motorcycle an almost reverent glance. "That is not just a *bike*. That's my custom Harley Road King, and she's built to perfection. A ton of blood, sweat and tears went into that beauty."

I bite back a smile at his protective overture toward the mass of steel. "So, is that a yes?"

"That's a yes. Do you ride?" Ash chuckles as he rakes a hand through his hair, his gaze fixed on me.

He needs to stop looking at me like that. It does things to me—all manner of things.

"I'm this big," I reply, holding my hand next to my head. "I couldn't even touch the ground on that thing."

"So, that's a no?" Ash volleys back.

"I've never been on a motorcycle. Not once in my life. Cue the shock and awe."

His dimples deepen as a smile stretches his face. "Unacceptable. We'll have to fix that. I'll take you on a real ride sometime, show you how much fun you can have."

"Didn't you already do that the other night?"

My cheeky aside earns a whoop of laughter from the man, and for a second, I forget I'm supposed to hate him.

He leans forward, dragging a finger along my jaw. "Once is never enough."

Oh, but it is, unless you have more favors that you need fulfilled.

Just like that, I remember why I must keep my distance. It's far too easy to fall prey to Ash's charming flirtations.

Far too easy to fall for him, period, and we all know where *that* got me.

I throw up my hands, offering him a shrug. "I'm asking because I didn't think you could jump a truck with a bike."

"Harley."

"Whatever."

Ash pulls a set of keys from his pocket and walks to the pickup parked directly across the lot from mine. "That's why I'm using Braden's truck."

"And also, why I asked Braden for help."

Ash pauses, a strange look flickering in his eyes. A flash of uncertainty crosses his features, though he quickly covers it. "Braden told me your situation, and I offered to come in his stead. Unless you'd rather wait for him."

"No. Thank you." I could keep arguing over this mundane detail, but let's be real—I'm only doing it to stretch out this moment in Ash's company, even if it means nothing to him.

Me and my stupid schoolgirl crush, twenty years post-graduation.

"Aren't you cold?" I ask, motioning to the thin t-shirt stretched across his chest.

He flashes another cocky grin, running a hand over his beard. "Not yet, but I'm sure I will be soon—unless, of course, you want to keep me warm."

Oh no, mister, you will not bait me with sexy flirtations, even if I started it. "You have plenty of women to fill that role."

Ash scoffs, shaking his head in frustration as his smile fades. "And yet, you're the one I'm asking. What does that tell you?"

Who the hell knows at this point?

I refuse to read into his words, because we both know that deep down, that's all they are.

Do they make me feel good? Of course, because that's exactly what they're designed to do.

But they don't mean anything more to Ash, and neither do I. A sad, but undeniable, truth.

Ash hops into Braden's truck, pulling it forward so the fenders are almost touching. Then he pops the hood and pulls the cables from Braden's backseat.

As he works, I notice the ink decorating his biceps, the lines vibrant beneath the glare of the streetlight.

The large design is an intricate mural celebrating the Roaring '20s—bold Art Deco patterns and sleek lines, with Gatsby's watchful eyes in the center, both haunting and mesmerizing. It's like staring into a world of glitz and illusion, a party that's already ended but still lingers in the air.

How did I not notice it before? After all, I have seen every inch of the man.

Brain, you've got to stop thinking about that night.

Reaching out, I trace the line of the tattoo, feeling Ash's muscles flex under my fingers. "This is a tribute to Gatsby."

He cocks his head, shooting me an appreciative nod. "See? I knew you'd get it. Most people think it's about Vegas for some reason."

"The eyes give it away," I murmur, aware that my fingers remain pressed against his skin, fingering the outline. "You really have always adored this time period."

Ash glances down at my hand, but he makes no move to pull away. "For as long as I can remember. It might seem stupid to some."

"Not me."

Ash pivots and wraps his hands about my waist, pulling

me close. "And because of you, it's now happening. The dream is coming true."

Don't read into it, Ori. Don't fall back into these feelings again, no matter how incredible he feels.

I shirk free of his embrace and offer a stilted laugh. "Nothing to do with me. I'm just the neighbor who gave you the go-ahead instead of grief."

He crosses his arms over his chest, his expression unreadable in the shadowy dark. "You're so much more than that."

My phone rings from inside my truck, pulling me out of the moment. I realize I'm now officially late for my dinner date. No doubt Roger is either making small talk with the hostess or teetering on the edge of a meltdown. "Shit. So much for being punctual. He's going to kill me."

"*He* better not," Ash grumbles, watching me carefully. "Where are you headed, anyway?"

"Out," I reply with a casual shrug.

"Out," he repeats slowly, as if tasting the word on his tongue. "That's all the info I get? Really?"

Wait a minute—did he just get snarky with me? Because if he did, he's about to regret it. I'm the queen of snark, and he'll wish he hadn't walked this path.

Especially after the events of the past week.

I shoot him a pointed glare. "Does getting a jump depend on that information?"

He pulls himself to his full height, which is imposing, if not a bit ridiculous, next to my diminutive stature. Then he locks his stony gaze on me, and despite the low light, there's no mistaking the storm in his verdant eyes. "Yes. If you're headed to the grocery store, no problem. But a date? That's a different story."

"You're joking."

"I am, but now I know where you're running off to tonight."

Ash's response leaves me with two choices: tell him the truth about my dinner plans or let him stew, wondering about my hot date for the evening. But here's what Ash doesn't know—it's not just Raven's snide comments the other day that have me on edge. No, that would be too easy, too petty for a woman my age. It was seeing him ride past my apartment that same night with some leggy woman clinging to him on the back of his bike, her arms wrapped around him like a lifeline. I have zero idea if it was Raven or some other member of Ash's roster, but for me, it was the last straw.

After that sighting, I'm fully embracing my pettiness. Let him sweat a little, though I'm sure he's already lined up at least one date for tonight. He is Asher Hammond, after all.

Releasing a soft grunt, I plant my hands on my hips. "I'm already late. Will you help me, or do I need to call AAA?"

An odd expression washes across Ash's face as he attaches the cables to the battery terminals. "Get in and start your truck."

I do as he asks, a relieved smile crossing my face when the engine turns over.

Ash detaches the jumper cables and lowers the hoods on both trucks before strolling to my driver's side window.

I lower the window, greeting him with a grateful grin. "Thank you."

He taps the roof of my truck, his jaw tight with tension. "No problem. You should have jumper cables up here, just in case. I'll grab you a pair the next time I'm out."

"You don't have to do that." I rub my hands together, blowing into them in a desperate attempt to warm my frozen fingers.

"I don't mind."

See? This is what I hate about Asher Hammond—the sweet, thoughtful side that completely contradicts his ruthless playboy reputation.

Fine, I *love* this side of him, but it messes with my head, and trust me, the man's already taken a blender to my emotions.

"Thanks for saving me, Mr. Hammond. You'll have to let me make it up to you."

Once again, the heat rises in my cheeks, fully aware of the double entendre of my words. Do I mean them? Who knows at this point?

Ash leans in through my open window, and his scent drifts over me—a heady blend of leather, cedar, and pure confidence that is unmistakably him and dangerously irresistible to my hormones.

I swear, the man gets within ten feet of me, and I damn near come on the spot, just from his proximity. He's obviously cast one hell of a spell on my body, and no matter how hard my heart tries to remind me that Ash is a terrible idea, my body isn't listening.

Which means I need to leave—immediately.

A task made more difficult by Ash's deliberate effort to prolong our conversation.

I peer over the top of my glasses, my mouth twisting into a half-smirk. "That depends. How would you prefer?"

I ask the question, though I already know the answer.

How indeed. My money's on a quick blowjob in the supply closet—when his harem isn't looking, of course.

Sorry, Ash, but that's not happening. Not after the other day. No matter how glorious your cock may be.

"Looks like you're the one who needs warming up." He grabs my still-cold hands, bringing them to his lips. His tongue teases along my fingertips in a soft, deliberate caress. "And as for making it up to me, I've got a ton of ideas when it comes to you."

That line should work, but all it does is arouse my fiery indignation. Because I don't just want another night with the man. I want *all* of them, and that isn't a possibility.

With a roll of my eyes, I pull my hands back. "Always comes back round to sex, doesn't it?"

He drops his hand to the windowsill with a hard sigh. "That's not what I meant."

Let's be real. It's *exactly* what the man means. He just doesn't enjoy being called out on it.

Time to steer this chat to neutral waters. "How about this? I'll pay you back in free coffee and baked goods for Black Lotus. Everything on the house for the next week. Be sure to take full advantage of all the goodies."

Ash's eyes widen at my segue. "While a thoughtful gesture, that is not necessary. How about you stay safe out there and I'll consider us even."

I force a smile and nod. "Fair enough."

What is wrong with me? I wanted to get off the sex talk track, but now I'm disappointed that he followed my lead.

See? This is why I need to avoid Asher Hammond, at least until this addiction to him ceases to be an issue.

My phone beeps with new texts, and I lean over to

retrieve it from its hiding spot on the passenger side floorboard.

I stifle a laugh as I flip through the myriads of messages. Roger is certain the hostess is plotting against him and if he has to order one more martini, he's not telling me all the gossip from the city.

After shooting him a quick-witted retort, I turn my focus back to Ash. "Sorry about that."

"He's impatient, huh?" Ash asks, clicking his tongue against his teeth.

"A bit, yes."

"Let him wait."

There's a forcefulness in his declaration that catches me off-guard. "Excuse me?"

But Ash ignores my response, choosing to focus on the inky darkness surrounding us. "You went home the other day without saying anything. I expected you to come back, and you just left."

Ah, yes. The holiday festival.

Heaving out a sigh, I realize there's no avoiding this conversation, even though I'm nowhere near ready to have it. My ego's still too raw to be rational.

I tap my finger against my mouth, debating the best way forward. "I figured you already had a full plate with all your friends. All your *fans*. You didn't need me tagging along, too."

He drums the windowsill, the aggravation apparent in his rigid stance. "Here's the thing. I wouldn't have asked you to go if I didn't want you there."

We can go round and round all night, circling the truth, but what's the point? I know why Ash slept with me, even if he'd rather eat glass than admit it.

Better to end this now. Let him know I know and be done with it.

I just wish saying the words out loud wasn't such a painful undertaking. After all, once I speak them, there's no more pretending.

I grip the steering wheel, calling upon every ounce of strength to get me through this without crying.

Universe, that's all I ask. Don't let me break down in front of him.

"I appreciate your help tonight, Ash, even if you don't approve of my destination. But listen, can we stop all of this?" I wave my hands around, desperate to corral my nervous energy.

His brow furrows. "Stop what?"

I close my eyes, releasing a long sigh as my hands come together in front of my lips, almost like a prayer. "You, acting like you like me. I've signed the lease, and I'll sign whatever additional paperwork you need, but please, stop insulting my intelligence with this charade. Okay?"

Anger flares in his face as he steps back from my vehicle. "What the fuck is that supposed to mean?"

Here goes nothing.

"I overheard you and your friend talking the other day. Discussing how you were willing to do anything, and apparently *anyone*, to get your speakeasy opened. That's why I left."

Ash tugs a hand through his hair, a perplexed look crossing his chiseled features. "*Who* are you talking about?"

Now he's going to pretend he doesn't remember? Cute.

"Raven, the Snow White-Jessica Rabbit mashup."

A flash of realization crosses his face, and he groans, rubbing his hand along the back of his neck. "I didn't think you heard that."

Wrong response, Ash.

I swipe a hand over my brow. "Well, I did."

"Raven is nosy as fuck, and I didn't want to get into details with her. I prefer discretion, remember?"

No, you prefer to keep enough distance between your ladies so that this is never an issue.

"Under normal circumstances, I'd agree. But when it comes to *that* topic, it would've been nice to know I wasn't just a cog in your wheel or worse, some inside joke. The least you could've done was to have that conversation in private. Do you think I hadn't already considered the possibility? I didn't need to hear you say it out loud."

"Ori, wait—"

But I'm done waiting. I've said my piece and now, it's time to return to life as it was before Asher Hammond.

I raise my hand to silence him as my phone pings with another text. "Don't worry about it, Ash. Seriously, I'm a big girl. But you hurt my feelings, and I choose to avoid people and situations that make me feel less than—because I'm fucking fabulous. Even if you don't agree. Now, I have to go."

"On another date." He spits out the words, the syllables hitting against the frost-ridden air.

Let him think what he wants. It doesn't matter, anyway.

I glance toward the entrance of Black Lotus and spy a lithe blonde shivering on the sidewalk, staring in our direction. "You'd better go. Your scantily clad public is waiting."

Ash tears his gaze from me, jerking his chin in greeting at the woman. "Fuck, I forgot she was coming tonight."

I'll bet you did.

That line seals the deal for me regarding Ash: game, set, match.

I laugh at the absurdity of the situation. "You know what? Instead of free coffee, I'll buy you a date book, so you can keep everyone straight and avoid any future awkward situations."

Ash throws up his hands. "Ori, it isn't—"

"Any of my business." Once again, I cut him off. I'm done hearing his excuses. I knew he was like this, and I can't act surprised now.

He's simply living up to his reputation, and what a reputation it is.

"Ash, are you coming inside soon?" the blonde woman calls from across the lot, running her hands along her arms. "It's freezing out here."

Ash rolls his shoulders, and I see him biting back his temper. "Which is why you should wait inside. I'll be right there."

"Go," I demand, shaking my head and shoving my phone into the safety of my purse.

But Ash moves closer to my truck, his fingers gripping my windowsill in a vise. "She's a client who's a nervous wreck about her first ink. She needs a lot of handholding."

"Look at how she's dressed, Ash. She's looking for a whole lot more than that."

"Why do you assume that?" he snaps.

I'm so over this game.

"Name one woman in this town who isn't after you."

Ash straightens and shoves his keys in his pocket, his face stormy. "That's easy. *You.*"

Chapter 19

All's Fair in Love and Coffee

Ori

"As a boss, you're amazing, but as a friend, you suck." Mina shoots me a mock glare from her seat on the bookstore floor.

My response? A casual shrug, since no amount of whining will get this task finished any faster. "Inventory is a necessary evil, Mina. Sorry it cut into our movie night. The sooner we get it done, the sooner we get to our beer and popcorn."

"That's not what I mean. Spill it, Ori. I've waited long enough."

"I hope you're going to clarify that statement."

"What happened between you and Ash?"

Christ. Not this topic again.

I groan and roll my eyes, determined to stay on course. "Nothing to tell. We got locked in the basement together and survived. Now, we're friends or … something. Next question."

Mina cocks a sculpted brow in my direction and I realize she will not let this matter drop. Not this time.

"Why do you think anything happened?" I ask, hoping my expression comes across as one of idle curiosity.

Mina holds up her hands, counting on her fingers. "Let me state the reasons. First, it's the way the man looks at you —though, to be fair, he's always done that."

I pause in pulling a book off the shelf. "Done what?"

"Stared at you. Like he couldn't quite figure you out, but you intrigued him."

"You mean glaring," I reply with a chuckle. "More than likely, he was plotting ways to kill me while I slept. Trust me, I shot him my fair share of glares, too."

"That's not it. It was so over the top, your contempt for one another, that everyone saw it for what it was."

I hate this game.

Releasing a heated sigh, I lean against the bookshelf and shoot her a withering look. "Which was what, exactly?"

"You two had a thing for each other. You wanted to hate each other and rip each other's clothes off in equal measure. That kind of passion is hot, and it's why I want *all* the details."

"Your crazy idea that us glaring daggers at each other equates to love might just be the silliest thing I've ever heard."

Mina shrugs, but I see the smirk playing on her mouth as she averts her gaze. "Of course, there's also the hickey you were sporting after your night together."

Damn, I forgot she saw that.

I groan and bite back a laugh. "That wasn't a hickey. It was …"

"An unprovoked vacuum attack?" Mina offers with a wide grin.

"Exactly," I reply, giving her a supportive wave. "Asher Hammond wasn't even in the room."

"Woman, you are full of shit."

"Think what you like. I know the truth."

"Exactly. A truth you won't share." Mina uncrosses her legs and folds over them in a stretch. "Not to mention how many times the man drops in for coffee every day. No one consumes that much caffeine."

Pushing my glasses up the bridge of my nose, I scan a few more titles, determined to appear unfazed by Mina's statement. "He's a busy guy. Takes a lot of energy to keep that train rolling."

"You would know."

"Honestly, he's only over here because we brew good coffee. Just ask him. He'll tell you the same thing."

"You two are brewing something else."

That's where Mina is wrong. There's nothing happening between Ash and me—especially after the other night, when I informed him we didn't need to pretend to be friends. Since then, he hasn't stepped foot into One More Page, or he's gotten great at avoiding me.

It's for the best. At least, that's what I keep telling myself. One day, my heart and head will agree and I'll be over my Asher Hammond crush for good.

Hopefully one day soon.

Mina smooths her pants, but the smug smile remains on her lips. "That, and Braden may have intimated something."

"Good old Braden," I mutter, realizing I've pulled the same book from the shelf three times.

"Plus, I was there when he pulled you into the supply closet, remember?"

We need a change of conversation *immediately*, or we'll never finish inventory and at this rate, my need for a drink increases exponentially with her every question. "Fine. You win. What do you want to know?"

"Was he magical?" She resumes her cross-legged stance, resting her chin on her hand as she gazes expectantly at me.

She has *got* to be kidding me.

"I'm not discussing details with you."

"So, he *was* magical. Knew it."

Pulling off my glasses, I pinch the bridge of my nose and count slowly to ten. "Mina, all the women in Sparkwood know this about Asher Hammond. It's the worst-kept secret in town."

"But it's different with you."

See, that's the trouble. It's no different with me. Not in the slightest. If anything, I drew the short straw. Some women in Sparkwood pique Ash's interest and earn themselves a regular spot in his rotation.

I was just a box to check off on his to-do list.

"Look, it was a one-night thing, okay? Was it fun? Absolutely. And yes, the man is ridiculously talented in bed. But the only difference between me and his harem of women is that what happened between us will never happen again."

End of story.

"I don't get it," Mina mutters.

I'm about ten seconds away from sprinting to the basement to grab my bottle of whiskey.

"Get what?"

"You had a great time with him. It's obvious he did, too."

"You heard him talking to Raven the day of the festival," I snap, losing my temper despite my best efforts. "You heard her *intimate* why Ash slept with me. You were there, Mina."

She raises her hands in surrender, realizing she's overstepped. "I also know he came looking for you after the festival and Raven wasn't with him. He was upset that you had left."

"Doubt it," I mutter. "He was just trying to save face. Nothing more. Look, I'm fine, okay? It's over and done with. Can we talk about something else?"

Mina nods, flipping on the radio. "How about some music? I can blast death metal and let you work out your aggravation that way."

Fuck it, I need to relax. Get a grip. Move on.

Chuckling, I shrug off the tension in my shoulders. "Death metal is never the answer, but I'm always up for some grunge. You know, *my* era of music."

Mina grins at my comment. "Deal."

A Pearl Jam song sounds through the speakers and I hum along, shaking off the malaise. It's hardly the end of the world and soon, I'll be lounging at Mina's with a cold brew and a rom-com.

It's going to be okay.

Hey, I get it. Mina's a fellow member of the diehard romantics club, and she held out hope that true love might blossom between sworn enemies—a real-life romance born from of one night of wild passion.

For a second, I did, too.

The rest of my staff couldn't care less if Ash and I made out, so long as we made up. Employees of both One More Page and Black Lotus are just relieved the war is over, that Ash and I can coexist in this shared space without the glares and muttered insults.

When our paths cross, we're friendly. Neighborly.

It's a far cry from our former relationship, but somehow, I think it's worse.

Worse, because I can't stop reliving my night with Ash—the feel of his mouth against mine, the weight of his body on top of me, his grizzly laugh, and the hint of a dimple when he smiles.

Worse still, because I know he used me to get my signature and I *still* fantasize about the man. That is some serious pull.

But I've counted three women in Ash's company this past week, and I'm sure I'm underselling him. There are seven nights in the week, and no doubt he's had a different beauty warming his bed for each one.

I'm long forgotten at this point.

So why can't I stop thinking about him?

Yes, our romp was epic, to quote my sex-sated self, but how many other women have used that term to describe Asher Hammond? Dozens? Hundreds?

What does it matter, anyway?

Somehow, despite my insistence that my heart not get involved in Ash's world, the damn organ refused to listen.

I feel something for him. Something I've never felt for any man.

Of all the men in the world, I fall for the one who's incapable of commitment. Incapable of loving beyond the carnal.

Oriana, you never fail to exceed expectations.

"Well, well, well, speak of the devil," Mina says from her perch on the ladder. "Ash is on his way over."

"Shit." So much for keeping my cool. I scramble to my feet, knocking over a few books in my haste. "Do me a favor —tell him we're closed, and he'll have to grab his coffee somewhere else tonight."

"What if he wants to talk to you?"

I wring my hands, desperate for the right words. *Any* words, at this point.

Sensing my nervous energy, Mina climbs down the ladder and pulls me into a hug. "Go into your office. I'll handle Ash."

All I can manage is a quick nod, eager to retreat to the safety of my inner sanctum. Motioning to the scattered books around us, I say, "And then head home. I'll meet you and the girls there for movie night."

"What about inventory?"

What about keeping quiet so I can escape to my office?

I wave my hand at the mess of books. "Tomorrow's another day, and the books aren't going anywhere. See you in an hour."

NOTE TO SELF: REFRAIN FROM HOLDING ANY VARIETY OF liquid item when flustered out of your mind. Without fail, you'll wind up wearing said item.

I blot at the coffee stain on my blouse, but it's a futile effort. With a sigh, I unbutton it and shrug it off. Best to leave that mess for the washing machine. Lucky for me, I came prepared with a change of clothes for movie night, and it's the epitome of high fashion—fleece leggings and a sweatshirt big enough to burrow into for the rest of winter.

At least I avoided engaging in stilted dialogue with the man who bartered orgasms for my signature.

Mina took one for the team.

I duck into the tiny bathroom adjacent to my office. It's no bigger than a broom closet, but it comes in handy during times like these.

A quick glance in the mirror reveals the wear of the last week. Funny how my night with Ash—whiskey-fueled and sleep-deprived—left me with pink cheeks and a healthy glow the next morning. Now, despite crawling into bed before ten every night, my eyes possess a deadened look, as if my soul is too tired to maintain the facade.

Maybe I just need a few good orgasms. I'll give my vibrator a spin later, even if it's a poor substitute. Honestly, it's like eating spam after dining on caviar—not even in the same universe.

Blowing out a breath, I shake off the despondency and turn on the faucet to wash my face. Nothing like frigid water to scare the horniness right out of you.

Over the sound of the running water, I hear my office door creak open before swinging shut.

That's strange. I guess Mina is still here.

"Mina, can you toss me my shirt from the bag in the corner?" I call out, drying my face with the hand towel hanging next to the sink.

But there's no answer.

Maybe I'm hearing things, or the ghosts have chosen tonight to make their presence known.

Dear God, let it be the first option.

I emerge from the bathroom, clad only in my bra and

pants, and cast a quick glance to the office door. "Hey, are you still here?"

"Depends on who you're looking for," a deep voice says to my right.

There, seated behind my desk with his hands casually folded behind his head, is Ash—wearing a devilish grin.

I jerk my hands to cover my tits. "Holy hell, you're not Mina."

Chapter 20

The Art of Not Falling

Ori

Ash shakes his head, but his smile never falters. "Incredible observational skills you've got there."

"How did you get in here?"

He points toward the door before leaning back further in the chair as his eyes travel the length of my body.

"Why are you smiling?"

Ash shrugs and bites his lip in that adorable fashion I love and hate in equal measure. "I'm admiring the view."

I can't be sure if it's the cocky glint in his eye or my grumpy disposition regarding the handsome playboy, but I'm done playing coy.

I hold my arms out from my body, ensuring he can drink in every inch of me. "Can I continue changing now?"

"Please do," he murmurs.

Don't get me wrong—his intense, fiery gaze is definitely affecting me, but I'll be damned if I let him know that.

The best way to handle a man like Asher Hammond? Act like his game is nothing I haven't played before.

"Suit yourself." With a shrug, I unbutton my pants and

wriggle out of them, barely containing my delight as he leans forward, resting his chin on his hand, clearly enjoying the show.

Come on, you'd do the same damn thing.

But when his hand drops below the desk and he adjusts himself with a grunt, I opt to take it up a notch. "You okay over there?" I inquire, my tone light and innocent.

"I love having a front-row seat to this striptease."

Typical response.

"Nothing you haven't seen before," I reply with a careless lift of my shoulders.

Ash gets up and walks around the desk, his boots thudding against the floor in measured steps. "Haven't seen that bra before. The other one was purple. Fucking nice, too."

I roll my eyes, desperate to maintain my equilibrium as he closes the distance between us. "Although I'm sure you've seen every variety of lingerie known to man, I was referring to what's underneath."

He glides his hands along my arms, sending a shot of sparks through me. "I will *never* tire of looking at those beauties. Most perfect tits on the face of the planet."

Again, it's a compliment of sorts, but I already know I have a nice rack. Besides, it's surface fluff—an interchangeable line that works on pretty much any woman.

Well, it won't work on me. Not anymore.

"You would know, Ash. You've sampled them all. Can I help you with something?"

He edges closer, leaning down to brush his lips against my ear. "You can help me with a lot of things. Where are you headed, anyway?"

Damn it, but he feels so good, his beard tickling my skin and sending a fresh wave of shivers down my spine.

I need space—desperately—between me and the small-town hottie of the year.

Shirking away from his touch, I grab the sweatshirt from my bag and pull it on. "I'm going out."

"With Mina?"

I know lying is wrong. I *know* this. But after this emotional rollercoaster of a week, I'm all about self-preservation. If that means knocking Ash's ego down a few pegs in the process, so be it.

I shrug, avoiding his gaze. "Nope."

His expression tightens as he crosses his arms across his muscled chest. "How many dates do you have in one week?"

He did *not* just ask me that question.

"Excuse me?" I snap, perching on a side chair to pull on my leggings. We need to end this chat, and fast. It's swiftly turning hazardous for my health.

He paces my office, his hands flexing as he walks. "Who is it this time? Plaid patches? Dead battery?"

I furrow my brow at the pointed questions flying from his mouth in rapid-fire succession. "What the hell are you talking about? Plaid patches?"

He halts in his pacing and turns to face me, the anger cutting lines into his face. "The fucking men you've been with this past week. I don't know their fucking names, nor do I care to know them."

Looks like Ash woke up and chose violence today. Well, I can play that game, too.

I march over to where he stands, arms crossed, and thrust two fingers under his nose. "Here are two answers for you. One, it's none of your damn business, and two, it's far less than *your* current weekly rotation. Trust me on that."

Ash tugs a hand through his hair, but he's not backing down. "That's a lie because I haven't been on any dates this week."

I hate playboys, but I hate liars more, especially when I've seen the man in action with my own two eyes. "What about your buddy, Raven? Or the little blonde outside your shop? How about the woman on the back of your motorcycle the other night? Want me to keep going?"

As soon as I speak the words aloud, I realize something. I sound a bit like a crazed stalker, knowing at least a percentage of the women Ash has hung out with in the last several days.

Then again, he seems to possess a list of my purported dates, as well.

Ash leans in, and I see the fire burning in his eyes. "What about you? There was that night at the bar with Kiki, the holiday festival where you ghosted me, and now there's tonight. The truth is, you've spent all this time running from me. The only time I actually kept hold of you was when I locked us in the basement."

I snap my fingers, recalling yet another member of Team Asher Hammond. "That's right. I forgot about the bartender—"

But I halt mid-sentence as his words sink in. Wait … did I hear him right?

Locked us in the basement?

Screwing my eyes shut, I freeze, shaking my head to clear it. "Hang on a second. You did what?"

Ash skews his mouth to the side as a faint hint of color climbs his cheeks. "Uh … yeah. About that night, I had a key to the basement door."

"You locked us in there intentionally? What if I had freaked out from being claustrophobic or something?"

"Obviously, if you'd freaked out, I would have opened the door. But I needed time alone with you without the rest of the world butting in."

Planting my hands on my hips, I offer a defeated shake of my head. "You really needed that signature, didn't you? Well, it worked. Congratulations."

He reaches out, grasping my fingers. "That isn't why, but can I ask you something?"

I stare at our intertwined hands, loving the look of his tatted digits enveloping mine. "Sure."

"Do you regret what happened between us that night?"

Of all the questions in the world, that was not on my bingo card. Cutting my gaze to his, I shoot him a tremulous smile. "I should, right? Protect my modesty and reputation in Sparkwood, since I'm the new girl in town and you are infamous for your storied history. But I don't regret that night. I had a good time with you."

He cocks a brow at me. "*Just* a good time?"

With a snort, I pull my hand from his grasp. "Please don't tell me your ego needs stroking. Don't you have enough local women to do that for you?"

"Answer the question."

Why not give him the truth, right? It's not like he doesn't know how talented he is in bed.

"It was phenomenal, okay? Perfection, if you must know. But you have made it abundantly clear that you don't agree with my opinion of that night's events."

"I've wanted you since the first day I saw you."

"Bullshit." I laugh out the word, knowing full well it's a

total crock, considering our initial meeting. "But thanks for the laugh."

Ash tips my chin up, forcing me to meet his gaze, dark and intense, those green eyes locking onto mine. "It's the truth. You have the most gorgeous mouth. First thing I noticed about you. Of course, then you opened it."

"Killing any attraction instantly." I bite my lower lip, desperate to rein in the laughter dancing in my throat.

Hey, at least I'm smiling again. Turns out, we both are.

"Hardly. Despite your best intentions and haughtiest attitude, you were still really fucking pretty."

There's that line again, and I enjoy hearing it tonight just as much as I did the first time.

Ash traces his finger along the shell of my ear, once again igniting every cell in my body. Then he reaches up and pokes at the pencil wedged in my hair. "Interesting hairstyle you've got there."

My temporary high crashes at his amused comment. For a second, I actually believed I was sexy and aloof. Silly me. I bet his dates never have pencils sticking out of a makeshift bun perched on their heads.

"What can I say? Library chic," I quip, trying to mask the sting.

In other words, the polar opposite of the buxom, scantily clad hotties who warm his bed every other night.

"You have beautiful hair," he murmurs, pulling his fingers through a loose strand. "You should wear it down more."

"I'll keep that in mind." I arch a brow at the handsome tatted man whose body I know so well. "As much fun as I'm having with this fashion critique, I highly doubt you came over here after closing just to comment on my hair. What's up?"

Ash shoves his hands in his pockets, rocking back on his heels. "Me and the guys are leaving tomorrow for a tattoo convention in Vegas. We'll be gone four days."

Ah, there's the *real* reason for him stopping by.

I plop down in the chair, reaching for my socks and boots. Best to end this conversation as quickly—and pain-lessly—as possible. "No worries, I'll grab your mail for you."

"Thank you, but that's not why I'm here."

Okay, I give up. "Then what do you need? You have more paperwork for me to sign or something?"

He perches on the corner of my desk, his foot tapping against the floor. "Is that what you think the other night was about? Your signature?"

"You tell me. Wasn't it?" Averting my eyes, I return my attention to lacing my boots. "That's what your girl Raven believes, anyway. She knew the reason you slept with me."

"She's not my girl, and she doesn't know a damn thing about me. My guess? She got jealous because of how I was looking at you."

I pause, tilting my head up to meet his gaze. "How was that, exactly?"

Ash shrugs offhandedly, but a smile threatens to break across his face. "Like I wanted to devour you whole. Something like that."

My entire body is now alight with tingles and sparks everywhere. Damn him, but that line felt so good.

So real.

Even if it's just his schtick.

"Ugh," I mutter, throwing in a roll of my eyes for good measure.

"What did I say now?"

"The right thing. The perfect response. As always. I swear, you're the Pussy Whisperer or something. Every comment hits—bang—right there, with all the feels." I motion toward my nether regions and huff out yet another sigh.

Ash doubles over, his laughter bouncing off every corner of the room. So glad I amuse him. "The Pussy Whisperer? That may be the best damn compliment I've ever received. I'm stealing that line."

"Go ahead. You've earned it. Countless times."

A grimace replaces his grin. Hell, I think he even winced at my words. "See? That's the trouble. When I look at you, all I'm thinking of is *you*. No one else. Just you. But you look at me and see every other woman I've been with throughout my life. So, yes, being called the Pussy Whisperer is one hell of an ego boost, but that's because I thought you were referring to yourself."

And now, I feel like an asshole, even if I highly doubt the sincerity of Ash's claim. Then again, why bother saying it at all?

I thrust out my hand, pointing toward him. "That right there is maddening. How can a man be so incorrigible, perplexing, aggravating, and adorable, all in the same breath?"

He dusts his nails along his shirt, that sexy smirk breaking across his oh-so-talented mouth. "Easy. I'm your Pussy Whisperer."

Now, it's my turn to fall back laughing. "You're not lying. There, are you happy now? I've admitted you're the greatest lover since the dawn of time. Anything else I can help you with this evening?"

"Yes." Ash resumes his pacing as a noisy sigh escapes his mouth. "My entire shop knows what happened between us, not that it's a secret."

"Meaning, they know we got locked in together or that we slept together?"

"Both, with an emphasis on the latter."

I chew my lower lip, shrugging in his direction. "Well, don't look at me. I didn't say anything. Besides, the billboard I ordered announcing our romp wasn't set to go up for another day."

That does it. Ash chuckles, shaking his head. "Always ready with a comeback."

"You said yourself I have a smart mouth."

"I said that you have a gorgeous fucking mouth. Extremely talented one, too."

His words set my entire body tingling, but I can't allow it. The man can't waltz in here and say things like this, only to leave tonight with a different woman.

Not happening, cowboy.

"Why are you telling me this bit of news? You want me to refute the rumor? Calm down your legion of women?"

"No. I don't know." His agitation kicks into high gear again as he picks up the framed photos on my desk, one by one. "But I'd like you to be honest with me."

"Okay."

"Who are all these guys you're dating?"

"What are you talking about?" Seriously, where are these supposed men? My overheated hormones would *love* to know.

"All the guys you've gone out with. Hooked up with.

Whatever," he replies with a grimace. "I know it's not my business, but I need to know."

I bark out a laugh, incensed at his accusations. Who does this man think he is? "Unlike you, I'm not on a quest to be the world record holder for most screws in a week."

"I already told you, Ori, that I haven't been out with anyone since our night together."

That's enough for tonight. Storming to my office door, I throw it open, jerking my chin toward it. "Please don't lie to spare my feelings. I saw those women with my own eyes. You're going to tell me you weren't sleeping with them?"

Ash holds up his hands, but doesn't make a move toward the office door. "Raven wanted to hook up, but I said no, because I wanted to hang out with you. The bartender got a hefty tip and a wave goodnight when I left right after you. The blonde chick cried throughout her entire session and drove me nuts. Who else am I missing?"

I roll my eyes, unsure *why* I continue playing this game with him. "The woman on the back of your motorcycle."

"When was that?"

"The night of the holiday fair. I live a mile up on Main Street and was checking my mail when I saw you at the light."

I'm trying to maintain an even keel, but Ash's behavior, combined with my bruised heart, is making that a remote possibility.

Ash narrows his gaze, running his hand over his beard as he tries to recall the woman in question. I hate knowing how delicious that beard feels against my skin.

"Jesus, are there *that* many women?" I bristle like a porcupine at the idea of another woman coming near him.

A fool's errand, I know, but tell that to my emotions.

Suddenly, his face splits into a grin. "You mean Jade."

"I don't know her name. I'm sort of shocked you can remember them all. Wait, did you buy a planner like I suggested? Organization is key," I grumble, the sarcasm dripping off every word.

His smile widens, and an infuriating chuckle emerges from Ash's perfect mouth. "You're jealous."

The bastard. "Are we done here?"

"No, I don't think we are." Ash moves toward me, but I duck away, intent on maintaining space between us. "Admit you're jealous."

"Get out, Asher."

He bites his lip, but another laugh escapes. "Jade is my cousin. She got stranded by her friend and needed a ride home. I helped her out because that's what family does."

I scan his handsome face, taking in the smirk playing on his lips and the amusement sparkling in his eyes. Part of me wants to grab him and kiss him senseless, while the other part of me is tempted to throw my cup of now cold coffee straight at his head. "I thought she was ... one of your women."

"Well, she's not. She's family. Glad to know you're jealous of other women in my space, though. I was starting to worry." He drifts a finger along my jaw, but I jerk my head away, earning another amused snort.

"Is that why you want to know about *my* dates?" Yes, I'm turning the tables on him and judging by the change in Ash's expression, I've hit the mother lode.

"Just curious," he mutters, averting his gaze.

Oh no, you're not getting off that easily.

I stand under him, peering into his now petulant face. "Just curious if I'm fucking them. Is that it?"

A muscle jumps in his jaw and I realize I'm not alone in this game. Ash is an equal player.

Now it's my turn to snicker—at us both, honestly. "Glad to know you're jealous of other men in *my* space."

"Not sure if you'd call it jealousy."

"What would you call it, then?"

Ash cracks his knuckles as his lips tighten into a thin line. "I'd like to have a chat with them. Back them the fuck up away from you."

Well, I'll be damned.

"Sounds like jealousy to me."

Ash resumes striding across the office floor and I wonder if he'll wear the boards out before the night is through. "Things are different since the other night. At least, they are for me. My employees are having a field day with this situation. Ribbing me mercilessly about us."

My heart sinks at his words. "They're making fun of me?"

"Of course not. They're making fun of *me*, because I swore I couldn't stand you, and now I'm inventing reasons to be near you."

I bite back a smile, forcing myself to appear unaffected. "You haven't been near me in days."

He scrubs his face with his hands, a look of aggravation coloring his features. "I know, because I don't want to like you, Ori."

So much for that warm and fuzzy feeling. Pushing my glasses up my nose, I throw up my hands in resignation. "Gee, thanks. Way to make a woman feel special."

Ash pushes the office door shut before backing me against the wall and caging me between his inked forearms. "I'm serious. You've messed with my brain, and now I can't stop thinking about you. *All the time.* A constant loop of your beautiful face, the feeling of being inside you, how you taste. I'm going out of my mind."

This time, the smile succeeds in breaking across my face. How can it not? I never thought I'd hear the man utter those words. "Asher Hammond, do you have a crush on me?"

Ash shakes his head, a snort of indignation rising from his chest. "Yes. Okay? I do. I have a crush on you. Fucking hell."

I tap my finger against my mouth, fearing I might melt from the intensity of the moment. "Let me get this straight. You like me, but you don't *want* to like me. You want to ignore me, but you can't. I'm fucking with all upcoming plans with other women. Am I close here?"

Finally, those green eyes meet mine, but instead of the usual flirtatious intensity, there's a softness lingering there. "Right on the money."

I can't believe he admitted it.

"Interesting." I bite my lip, gazing up at him through my lashes. "Here's my take on your predicament. I want you to like me, and I'm not sorry in the slightest that you do. I hope the image of us together is burned into your brain the way it's burned into mine. As for other women, please don't make me go to jail for killing them. I don't look good in stripes."

His laughter punctuates the air as he frames my face with his hands, pulling me into a fierce kiss. His tongue melds with mine in a slow, coaxing rhythm and a low groan rises from his chest as he presses his body to mine. Just like that first night, I feel the desire coursing through him. Coursing through us both.

The difference? This time, I believe it's real.

Rising on tiptoe, I grip his shoulders, desperate to feel every inch of him. I want more. Hell, I want *everything*.

"Greedy little minx," he breathes against my mouth, nibbling my lower lip. "What am I going to do with you, woman?"

With a wink, I wrap my arms around him, snuggling into his embrace. "I can think of a ton of things. I deserve it after a shitty week."

He pulls back to shoot me a confused look. "What happened?"

"*You* happened, Asher Hammond. After all your women—"

"They're not my women," he grunts.

"I only learned that piece of information five minutes ago. I spent the last week ruminating on it. Trust me, my head wasn't a good place to be."

"Time to get you out of your head, so whatever bullshit plans you have tonight, you're canceling them."

"Am I?" I ask, giggling when he buries his head against my neck.

"Yep. You're spending the night with me in our favorite basement. Trust me, I will make this week end on a high note." He drags his tongue along my skin, delivering a series of gentle nips to my throat.

"Don't you dare leave another mark."

"No promises," he murmurs, his teeth raking against my flesh. "Go ahead. Cancel your plans."

"Why would I do that?" My voice is low as my fingers trace along the planes of his chest, desperate to rip every stitch of clothing from his body.

Ash meets my gaze with a cocky smile. "Simple. Because you like me—a whole fucking lot."

Truer words have never been spoken, and it's an idea that equally terrifies and excites me.

"Is that a fact?" I ask with a roll of my eyes.

"Yes, but I like you even more than that. Okay?"

That settles it. My heart doesn't stand a chance.

I flash him a coy grin while trailing my nails across his cock, earning a grunt of approval as he bucks against my hand. "You have the key this time?"

He smirks at me. "I had a key the last time, remember?"

I hold out my palm. "Give it here." When he hands me the key, I tuck it into my bra. "This time, I'm locking *you* in."

"Woman, I'd go willingly."

God, I love how that sounds so damn much.

"Let me call Mina."

Ash's eyes widen. "Wait a damn minute. Is that who your plans were with?"

I motion to my outfit. "You think this is appropriate attire for a date night?"

He chuckles, running a hand across his jaw. "She didn't say a word. Give me your phone. I'll break the news to her."

"It's on the desk."

Ash captures me in another heady kiss before grabbing my phone. "Hey Mina, it's Ash. Here's the thing. I'm stealing your boss for the night. We have some very important negotiations to go over and her sexy ass will be tied up for hours."

My mouth drops open as he hands me the phone. "You

know she's going to be all over that statement, right? There is no way I can hide this from her now."

Ash shrugs. "Let's give them something to talk about."

"Fine, but make it amazing, because you owe me." I smile as he steals another kiss, knowing I'm a marshmallow against this man.

"Let the Pussy Whisperer work his magic."

I snort out a laugh at his cocky aside. "Do you think another night of great sex is going to cure what ails me?"

"It's a damn fine start, but then, after I get back from the convention, I have another plan."

"Really?"

He wraps his fingers around my wrist, pressing a soft kiss to my pulse point. "Have dinner with me, then I'll get my fill of dessert."

I cock a brow at him. "You mean a date?"

"Yes."

A shiver races down my spine and I'm sure he feels my pulse bounding against his lips. "You don't date."

"First time for everything, Ori." Ash sighs, but the happiness on his face is evident. "And for you, I'd try anything."

Epilogue: Into the Flames

Ash

Ori stands before me, hands on her hips, smirk on her lips, and I know the woman will be the death of me.

But hey, I'll sure as hell die happy.

"Come on, Little One. I'm tired of waiting." I extend my hand, biting back a smile when her fingers grasp mine.

Look, despite my claims to the contrary, I don't hate the concept of romance. Hell, there was a time when I loved the idea.

But now, loving someone lies beneath a million layers of regrets, dumb choices, and painful memories, and, despite my insane attraction to this tiny bookworm, I'm not looking past tonight.

One day at a time has a whole new meaning where I'm concerned.

Somehow, I think she gets that fact.

"I'll meet you downstairs," she replies with a wink. "I have to turn off the stove in the store."

What she doesn't know is I have no intention of letting

her out of my sight. This woman is aces at disappearing and if I don't fulfill this aching need soon, I'm going to lose my mind. "Lead the way."

Ori strolls ahead of me into the store, and I can't help but admire her luscious hip shake and firm, round ass.

Fuck, it's perfect.

"Keep shaking that gorgeous peach, and I might just take a damn bite out of it."

Ori glances back at me, throwing a flirty wink at me over her shoulder. "Promise?"

"Get over here." With a laugh, I grab her about the waist and toss her over my shoulder in a fireman's hold. Then I give her ass a playful smack before sinking my teeth into the soft fabric of her leggings.

Ori lets out a squeal of surprise, laughter bubbling up as she playfully pushes against my back. "Just wait until I get my hands on you, Asher Hammond."

I tighten my grip, delivering another smack to her rear. "Maybe it's my turn to play."

"Please do," she murmurs, reaching out her hand toward the wall. "Damn it, I can't reach the off switch from here."

"Actually, leave it on." I gently lower Ori from my shoulder, letting her slide down the front of my body until her feet touch the ground.

"Don't you want to go downstairs?" Ori asks, wrapping her arms around my waist and propping her chin on my chest to shoot me a mischievous smile. "I thought it was playtime."

I chuckle and pull her flush against me, loving how she melts into my embrace. "Trust me, I plan on playing all night."

"What about Vegas?"

I shrug, sliding my hands beneath her leggings to palm her booty. "I'll sleep on the plane after you wear me out."

Ori shakes her ass. "What are we waiting for, then? Let's go."

But I don't want to rush this moment, or any moment, with her. In her arms, the world makes sense, even for a few brief moments.

I can't explain it. I'm not sure I'm ready for a woman like Ori, or that I'll ever hit that milestone, but damn it, I want to try.

Most of all, I want her to know that our night together had nothing to do with her signature. Sure, that's the reason I locked her in the basement, but once I broke through her defenses, I knew one thing—I never wanted to let her go.

So, despite her insistence, I'm taking my time with her tonight.

"Change of plans," I say, earning a wide-eyed glare from my petite woman. "Not like that, Little One. You look fucking gorgeous in the firelight. I'm enjoying the view."

Although, I'd like to see her wearing nothing but the smile I gave her.

Ori pivots to face me, her teeth catching her lower lip, eyes dark with intent. Then, with a devious little smile, she trails her fingers down my chest before giving me a gentle shove, pushing me into the leather armchair behind me. I sink into the seat, unable to look away as she steps closer, her gaze daring me to make the next move. "You want me to do all the work tonight, don't you?"

"Fuck no. Get over here and I'll gladly take over." I crook my finger at her, smiling when she straddles my lap.

"Better?" she whispers, her breath catching when I

anchor my hands on her hips and pull her down against my cock.

"Getting there." I glide my thumb along her lower lip, my breath hitching as she swirls her tongue across the tip. My hand wraps around the back of her neck, pulling her closer as I capture her luscious mouth in a fierce, hungry kiss.

Ori grinds against me, her hips moving in a provocative dance as they bid me to play. I wrap my hands around her ass and thrust against her, feeling the desperation build when she scratches her nails across my back.

"I thought we weren't leaving marks," I tease, nipping at the soft skin of her throat, the hint of honey and jasmine wreaking havoc with my senses and drawing me deeper into the moment.

"Something to remember me by," Ori answers, her voice a husky moan as she threads her fingers through my hair.

"There's no way in hell I could forget you." My hands slip beneath her shirt to cup her breasts, my thumbs teasing across her nipples.

I need to get her downstairs—now. Hell, at this rate, I'll end up taking her on the stairs, too. If she wants to play, I'm ready for it.

"Wait for a second." Ori mumbles as she scrambles off me, breaking the heat of the moment.

What the hell? Am I missing something?

"Where do you think you're going?" I grunt as I loosen my jeans and adjust myself.

I don't have to wait long for an answer.

Ori lifts the hem of her shirt and drops it to the floor. Then she shoots me a playful grin as she unhooks her bra and slides it down her arms before tossing it aside with a mischievous wink.

The firelight plays off her every curve, throwing golden shadows across the planes of her stomach and the curve of her breasts.

She's so damn beautiful—and totally exposed to all of Sparkwood, I realize with a start.

"You know your store has a big fucking window that fronts on Main Street, right?" I ask the question, although I'm sure as hell not stopping this spur-of-the-moment striptease.

Two times in one night from the woman who's commanding my every thought—yes, please.

Ori shrugs and leans against a bookshelf to pull off her boots and socks. "I'm aware."

I smirk at her nonchalant attitude toward public exposure, loving this side of Oriana. "So, the whole town gets a free show tonight?"

She releases a husky and wicked laugh as her fingers toy with the waistband of her leggings. "'Tis the season, right?"

I've had countless women offer up their personal brand of strip downs, but there's something about Ori that blows them all away. She looks every inch the prim and proper lady, one who might crochet on winter nights and attend Sunday service. But that's where the similarities end, because underneath her good girl persona lies the greatest seductress I've ever known.

"That gift belongs to me," I reply, my voice charged with emotion. "Now, come here and let me unwrap it."

"Patience, sir." She strips off her leggings and underwear, standing before me in all her naked perfection. Her ivory skin glistens as she pivots slightly, tossing a naughty smile my way.

I'm going to blow my load in my pants if she waits any longer.

"Right now." Maybe it's the growl in my voice or the edge of possessiveness plying the words, but Ori obeys my command, once again sitting astride my lap.

I slide my hands along her sides, her skin softer than spun silk beneath my palms. "You're playing with fire, Ori."

She leans in, her voice a smoky whisper at my ear. "You're the one who wanted to stay close to the flames, Ash. Maybe I want to burn, too."

I crash my mouth against hers, my fingers digging into the meat of her thighs as I try to rein in my last vestiges of control.

But Ori enjoys driving me to the brink of madness, her tongue teasing mine in a slow, seductive dance as she grinds her sweet pussy against me.

"Lose the pants," she murmurs, her mouth warm and wet on my neck, every touch stoking the firestorm inside me.

"You really want to give Sparkwood a show tonight, don't you?" I grunt, sliding my fingers inside her heat as my thumb teases her clit.

Ori looks over the top of the chair to the street beyond. "It's empty. Not a soul in sight. But, should someone take a notion to peer in here, all they'll see is me. They won't see you. So, it's a win-win situation."

"How is that a win-win?" Hell, even those few words require a tremendous effort, when all I can think about is burying myself inside her and claiming every curve.

She leans back slightly before taking another peek out

the window. "You take me on the ride of my life and no one but us is the wiser about the conductor driving this train. That way, we *both* have an amazing time."

Fuck that noise.

I tangle my hand in her hair, forcing her to meet my gaze. "Little One, I'll carry you to that front window right now. Then I'll press your naked body against the glass, wrap my hands around your gorgeous hips and take you from behind—right there, for the whole damn world to see."

Those huge dark eyes widen behind her lenses, but she's not backing down from my challenge. "You wouldn't."

"Try me," I growl, my thumb grazing her jawline as I tilt her head up to feel her pulse hammering beneath my fingers. "I'll make you scream so loud they'll hear you in the next town over. But *everyone* will know who's bringing you that level of pleasure."

Ori digs her fingers into my shoulders and whimpers, her movements growing more frenzied by the second.

"Everyone will know you're mine." My words are a low rumble, my brain not latching onto their deeper meaning—my body not giving a damn.

She slides to her knees at my feet and fumbles my belt open, but her eyes never waver from mine. I lift my hips as she tugs my pants down.

Sparkwood residents want to watch? Fucking let them.

I'm too lost in Ori to care.

With a coy smile, she wraps her slender hand around my cock and lowers her head to taste me, gliding her tongue over my shaft. I buck against her mouth as she works me over, teasing every inch of me and pushing me to the brink of madness.

Fuck, but this woman gives the greatest head—and she damn well knows it—but there is no way I'm coming anywhere but inside her. "Get your gorgeous ass up here."

Ori scratches her nails along my thighs, taking a few extra seconds to tease the tip of my cock before climbing on top of me. "What do you need?" she murmurs.

"You. Just you." I slide my cock along her slick skin, her desire coating my tip and driving me out of my fucking mind.

She's the only cure for this out-of-control addiction. I'm a fiend for her—the feel of her, the taste of her—everything about this woman drives me wild in the best way.

Then I hear the familiar sound of the condom wrapper and realize I was about to take Ori raw.

Something I still *desperately* want to do.

Look, I'm always careful—every single time. I never slip up with slipping on protection because you don't know where someone has been. No matter what they claim.

But this time, I got so lost in her—and the moment—that I forgot everything else.

"Fuck. Damn near forgot that," I grumble as she rolls the latex down over my shaft.

"Now *that* would be playing with fire," Ori replies with a wink.

I reach up, cupping her face, and smile when she delivers a gentle nip to my palm. "Maybe you're not the only one who wants to burn."

She answers me by sliding down my length as I grip her ass and thrust inside her core.

A low moan escapes my mouth as her pussy tightens around me, milking my cock. She's so fucking tight and wet, and I can't get close enough to her heat. I breathe in as the scent of her arousal fills me and claim her mouth with my own to swallow her whimpers as she rides me.

She feels too good. So damn perfect as she writhes against me, her movements becoming more and more desperate as her body shakes.

"Ash, Ash—" she cries, her fingers digging into my shoulders.

Her need only spurs me further as I piston inside her, each passing second more primal than the last.

Her body jerks, but I won't give her a moment's reprieve. I feel the pleasure rip through her as her nails scratch into my skin, inking me with a new brand of tattoo.

Ori collapses against me, her breathing heavy and panting. "You. Are. Amazing."

A wicked smile tugs at my lips as I hold her tighter, feeling her pussy quiver around me. "That's just round one, beautiful, and I've got all night."

A contented purr escapes her lips. "Aren't I the luckiest girl in the world?"

"Not yet," I murmur, nuzzling her throat. "But you will be. One day, I'm claiming all of you."

Her eyes flash with a thrill that matches my own, but she only presses harder against me, a challenge in her gaze. "Then you better be ready for the heat, because I don't do anything halfway."

As she resumes her rhythmic flow, chasing the dragon for an even greater release, I realize something—Ori is *my* dragon, the rush I can't resist, the one that delivers every time.

But what happens when she pins me with those dark, all-seeing eyes and demands everything? The romance, the happily ever after. She deserves it all. More than I can probably give.

What if I'm not built for forever? What if the lacerated pieces of my heart are too damaged, too scarred to be whole? What if ...

The answer slices through all my doubts, silencing every question—none of it matters, because I can't let her go.

And that idea terrifies me most of all.

"Hey," Ori's voice breaks through, soft but steady, pulling me back to her. "You with me?"

And just like that, I am.

The End. For now.
But don't worry—Ash and Ori have plenty more
unfinished business waiting for you.

Preorder Your Copy of Chasing Sparks Today!

Want a Bonus Scene with Ash in Vegas?
There's some serious drama cooking on the other side of
the country. Free when you sign up for my newsletter!

Also by M.L. Broome

Make You Stay

Friends to Lovers / Opposites Attract / Single Dad

And Then Came You

Friends to Lovers / Slow Burn / Celebrity Romance

Both Sides Now

Young Widow / Forbidden Romance / Love After Loss

Forgot to Tell You Something

High Angst / Surprise Pregnancy / Medical Romance

Hook Up

Brother's Best Friend / Sports Romance / He Falls First

A Sinner's Memory (Lyrical Love Letters)

Rockstar Romance / Second Chance / Single Dad

Alchemy Unfolding

Reverse Age Gap / Sexy Surfer / Medical Romance

A Series of Moments Trilogy Box Set

High Angst / Celebrity Romance / Medical Romance

Yuletide Acres

Yule Holiday Romance / Second Chance / Single Dad

It Must Have Been the Mistletoe

Christmas Romance / Second Chance / Snowed In Together

Keep in Touch!

Want important announcements, bonus goodies and exclusives, and behind the scenes peeks at my real life? Subscribe to my twice monthly newsletter!

Want preorder and new release alerts? Follow me on Amazon and Bookbub!

I'm always posting snippets from my books and upcoming releases on Tiktok, Facebook and Instagram. Be sure to follow me there!

About the Author

M.L. Broome is a bohemian spirit with a New York edge. She writes high-octane contemporary romance with plenty of angst and steamy, sexy goodness. Her characters are bitingly real, earning their happily-ever-after only after some emotional ass-kicking and personal growth.

When M.L. isn't writing or holding one-sided arguments with her characters (spoiler alert—they always win), she loves losing herself in nature on her micro farm, one of her rescue buddies by her side.

She adores dressing up and kicking back, a glass of whiskey with an equally stunning view, and experiences that make the soul—and senses—tingle.

For all the latest releases and exclusive goodies, subscribe to M.L. Broome's newsletter today at https://www.mlbroome.com.

www.ingramcontent.com/pod-product-compliance
Lightning Source LLC
Chambersburg PA
CBHW030000010826

48973CB00007B/2098